MARGARET LEECH (1893-1975) was born in Newburgh, New York. After completing her preparatory education at private schools in Newburgh and Poughkeepsie, Margaret Leech entered Vassar College and in 1915 received her B.A. degree. In the fall of that year she went to New York City to work for the Condé Nast publishing company, writing trouble-shooter letters to subscribers who complained about not receiving their copies of magazines.

During the 1920s, Leech was chiefly occupied with writing novels. Her first novel, *The Back of the Book* (1924), is a story about a young office girl in New York. *Tin Wedding* (1926) concerned the thoughts and feelings of a woman on her tenth wedding anniversary. With *The Feathered Nest* (1928), a study of possessive mother love, she added what has been called another "panel in a screen of American family life."

In 1935 she began writing historical works, which became her vehicle to fame. *Reveille in Washington, 1860–1865* (1941), a comprehensive view of the nation's capital during the Civil War, and *In the Days of McKinley* (1959), a study of President William McKinley and his times, each won her a Pulitzer Prize in history.

Margaret Leech was married to Ralph Pulitzer on August 1, 1928. As an author in her own right and as the wife of the publisher of the New York *World* (his father, Joseph Pulitzer, had founded the Pulitzer Prizes), she belonged to a distinguished literary circle that included publishers, playwrights, actors, journalists, and other writers. Collaborating with Beatrice Kaufman, she wrote her only play, *Divided by Three*, in which Judith Anderson starred in the fall of 1934.

TIN WEDDING

by

MARGARET LEECH

SHORELINE BOOKS

an imprint of

W · W · NORTON & COMPANY · NEW YORK · LONDON

Published simultaneously in Canada by Penguin Books Canada Ltd,
2801 John Street. Markham, Ontario L3R 1B4
Printed in the United States of America.

Library of Congress Cataloging-in-Publication Data

Leech, Margaret, 1893–1974.
Tin wedding.

I. Title.
PS3523.E347T56   1986   813'.52   86–146

ISBN 0-87140-141-X

W. W. Norton & Company, Inc., 500 Fifth Avenue, New York, N. Y. 10110
W. W. Norton & Company Ltd., 37 Great Russell Street, London WC1B 3NU

1 2 3 4 5 6 7 8 9 0

TIN WEDDING

TIN WEDDING

CHAPTER I

i

THE house, high and narrow, of red brick, with
facings of white stone, was not greatly different
from its fellows, which stretched in an even, dignified row, as yet uninvaded by apartment houses,
between Park and Madison Avenues. Its singularity
lay in a freshness, a gay and finished perfection.
The brasses of the doorway were brilliantly polished, the vestibule shone with ivory-colored paint.
Awnings, patently new, fluttered vivid stripes of
white and green; and from the fine iron railings
which bordered the French windows, ivy fell in
vigorous showers of glossy leaves.

The outer doorway was framed by two stone
pillars, which supported the shallow balcony on
which opened the windows of the living room.
These were flung wide to the mild May morning;
and the housemaid, her dust-cloth at her hip, could
be seen moving inside, before she came to lean in-
quisitively out. With an air at once transient and
deliberate, she examined the car at the doctor's
house across the way; noted the delivery boy trun-
dling his hand-cart near the curb; and, on whisk-

9

ing into the house, cast a swift look to left and right—westward toward the streaming traffic brightened by the enamel-green of buses, eastward toward the stark parallels of the elevated roads, striping the gray perspective of street.

For a moment, the house was impenetrable; only the awnings gently wavered, only the ivy stirred. Then a little golden boy appeared on the narrow balcony of the fourth floor. He wore his small, mannish shirt and drawers. His body was slight and finely formed. He stood on tiptoe—he was seven—and peeped over the ivy boxes until he could see below him a balcony of the adjoining house, on which a parrot had been set to take the air in a large gilt wire cage. Slowly he lowered a long string, to which he had tied a painted iron horse and, carefully, his yellow head intent, he knocked the horse against the cage. Again and again he thumped the cage; again and again the parrot ruffled its feathers and sputtered and squawked. The little boy chuckled; evidently, it was a pleasant game. Then a thin hand appeared at the window, and he was dragged unceremoniously within.

ii

Like a nicely adjusted mechanism, the routine of the house went forward. There was an orderly bustle in the kitchen. In the dining room the breakfast table was set, the morning papers laid at Mr. Fanning's place, the heater arranged on the side-table, the curtains drawn just a trifle. On the floor above, the housemaid now went quickly to and fro with wide bowls of flowers. An elderly maid descended to the pantry where the yawning hampers waited, for Mrs. Fanning would go to her country house in less than a week. A red-haired woman bore upward a tray laden with yellow Spanish pottery and a silver mug of milk.

The living room and library, facing each other across a broad hall, lay gleaming with immaculate order, waiting for the day to begin. It was not for the passing of the servants that they had been made beautiful. Costly rugs shone somberly on their waxed floors, and only a connoisseur could have told the value of the dim Chinese painting above the library mantel. There were lovely colors and gracious fabrics. The curtains were long, crisp, ruffled—the curtains which are made by expensive decorating shops. The walls of the library were serried rows of books, and on the many tables were more books, were bowls of flowers and shaded lamps and colored boxes for cigarettes and ashtrays like shallow jewels. There were small bright Chinese bottles and many cunning carvings—rabbits of jade; cornelian frogs; fat amethyst ducks; a primitive, spirited horse of rose quartz; and, solitary between the flowers on the living-room mantel, a tall crystal goddess, a gracious lady of ice, so cool, serene and smooth.

These were not austere rooms. They were elegant, but they were also gay, almost with a touch of frivolity; rooms arranged, it was clear, by a woman, one who delighted in the possession of lovely and amusing things.

iii

Over the living room was Jay Fanning's bedroom, plain of walls and rugs and curtains. It held a desk and a long table, piled with books and papers, and littered with a man's paraphernalia: mounting packages of cigarettes and matches, tobacco, a brass bowl filled with pipes, field glasses, a pair of boxing gloves. There were photographs: his mother and father, faded and brownish in a worn frame; his brother on a fishing trip; his wife, a slender bride, all wide dark eyes; his son at several ages. His dinner clothes had been flung on an easy chair, and beside them sprawled a weary shirt, pierced with onyx studs.

The covers of the bed were tossed, the pillow was rumpled. The green-shaded lamp on the bedside table still burned with a sickly light. Near it a book, cast face-down, had tipped the ashtray, scattering a profusion of cigarette stubs. Now Jay Fanning started, turned on his pillow, his eyelids quivering. But this was to be a holiday. He was not going downtown this morning. So he fended off the moment of waking, pushed it from him and slept again, sinking into the deep slumber which sometimes comes to light sleepers in the late morning—a thick, warm unconsciousness which the sunlight, spilling over the foot of his narrow bed, was powerless to disturb.

iv

Lucia Fanning lay across the hall, in the room at the back of the house. Draperies of soft, heavy silk, rose-pink, were half-drawn against the morning light. Rose-pink, too, were the full skirts of her dressing table, the top of which was a shining mirror, on which rested her delicate boxes and bottles and a pair of blue and gold vases, filled with pansies. The low boudoir chairs were covered with an old French printed cotton, portraying in a lively pattern of pink and white the nice activities of virtuous children.

One of the two beds in the room was politely decked with the silk coverings appropriate to daytime. In the other, Lucia slept. But she stirred gently, uneasily, as though she were eager to awake, warned by some small, faithful timepiece within her that it was time to put out her hands to the new day. Still, while the street noises trickled faintly between the rose-pink draperies, she continued to sleep; still, her husband slept, across the hall. Their house was smoothly administered in the small rou-

tine of the morning. It was her house; she had
planned it. It was his house; he had paid for it.

v

The shade whispered sharply against the window,
and Lucia Fanning opened her eyes to the shifting
pattern of sunlight on the floor. Between the curtains she could see the radiance of the May morning.
A lovely day!

She was tired, of course, she must be terribly
tired, for they had come home late from Eva
Tailer's party. But she was out of bed in an instant,
she thrust her feet into the cool silk of her mules
and ran across the floor to her bath. She was in
haste to bathe and dress, yet she could not resist
pausing for a moment to open the window and lean
out into the cool, delicious morning. The breeze
touched her cheek, blew a lock of hair across her
forehead. She saw, above the high, uneven roofs,
the clean blue sky. It was a perfect day. What
is so rare . . .? No, that was June. But no June
day could be lovelier than this. That was a superstition, anyway, about June, a *cliché*. . . .

Her hand lay on her throat, and under it she could
feel her breast, rising, falling quickly. She was
stirred by her emotion, her expectation; lightly
shaken, as though the soft morning air could ruffle
her heart-beats. After all her hopes and prayers
for this day . . . it was almost unbelievable that

it should be so fine, such a perfect day for a holiday.
It was almost as if her feeling of its importance had
received official sanction. Thank you, thank you,
she breathed impulsively. But she told herself that
she was being silly; and, with tears pressing at her
eyes, she tried to smile at her emotion. It was the
season of the year, she was always sentimental in
the spring, and nothing was more moving than the
reticent, shy loveliness of spring in the city. The
very fragrance of May rose to her window, above
the rustling, accelerated hum of traffic; and, leaning
over the sill, Lucia saw the tulips in her garden,
impudent clowns posturing against the dusty brick
of the house in back.

With a sudden impatient movement she left the
window, and began to prepare for her bath. Last
night every one had admired her gold lace dress;
rather an affected dress, she admitted, cut very
low, with long, tight sleeves. Jay had thought she
looked well. She always knew when Jay thought
she looked well. Even when he said nothing, she
recognized that expression in his eyes which indicated approbation, told her that he was proud of
her.

They had been very gay, dining at the Marigny
with Adrian and attending the opening of a play
designed for the diversion of summer visitors to
the city—a palatable farce in which Jay had a financial interest. After the theater, they had gone to
Eva Tailer's. Oddly, Lucia paused to consider, it

was customary to think of that house as Eva's, rather than Mark's. Perhaps this was because Eva, as a successful novelist, was the more colorful of the two; perhaps, because Eva herself set the fashion of disregarding Mark. Lucia often found herself in a world where acceptance of marriage difficulties or ennuis was philosophical, even wholehearted. Eva always seemed to her cynically indifferent to the widening breach in her relation with her husband; and Lucia confessed that possibly a distaste for this attitude had made her wish to avoid the party last evening. But Jay had been evidently anxious to go, so she had made no objection.

From the glass on the toilet table she took the gardenias she had worn. Always she kept her gardenias in water overnight, hoping for a miracle, though she knew how it was with gardenias. Strange, she thought, diverted for a moment, how we delude ourselves with false little hopes. Next time I will keep them again, she acknowledged, smiling, though she saw that the flowers were, like all the others, quite brown. She held them for a moment, breathing their rank sweetness. Gardenias suited her, for she was very pale; not with a lavender-tinged blonde whiteness, but with the warm pallor of a black-haired woman.

She laid the flowers regretfully aside. How thoughtful Jay was! In his punctilious and graceful

courtesy, he far surpassed the other men she knew.
And I have done my part, too, she said to herself.
Especially at the beginning, there were many little
adjustments to make. That is always so, that is
only natural. Our marriage has been happy because
we have both been determined to make it so. I
have done everything— . . . But, her throat con-
tracting painfully—she was absurdly tired, they
should not have stayed out so late—she turned to
safer thoughts. Spreading a thin cream over her
face, she admitted that she was still a young woman,
only thirty-two, and her face was as lovely as ever;
if not with the bright bloom, the luscious, peach-like
glow of youth, then with a compensating depth of
interest, a lilied distinction, a poignant delicacy.
She did not have to worry on the score that she had
faded. Jay admired her, there was no doubt of
that; he was always paying her charming compliments. Many men still found her disturbing,
though for some tastes she had always seemed too
reserved, too lacking in animation—she had a
fastidiousness which forbade casual flirtations.
Since the birth of her son, she had not been strong;
but even in her nightgown it was possible to see how
much distinction she had, how *soignée* she must
look when she was dressed. Her small, erect head,
the graciousness of her shoulders, her slender hips
and the long, narrow bones of her hands and feet
gave her a natural elegance.

vi

The warmth of the bath did not tempt her to relax, but rather emphasized the impulse of haste which possessed her. For now she felt clearly the tremor of excitement which she had discerned rising and falling under her hand, as she stood at the window. It ran along her veins and pressed upon her throat, a disturbing elation, an expectancy that was almost pain. And she looked at her dressing case, open on the chair, waiting for its bottles. Rachel had packed it the night before; it was ready, all but the toilet things. Peering from the tub, she could see her underwear, her dressing gown, nicely folded. Ah, but the nightgown—that was not the right nightgown. Still, she couldn't expect Rachel to know about that.

Her bath completed, she soaked a piece of cotton in cold water, pressed it thin and damp between clasped palms. Then, sitting down at the toilet table which stood by the window, she wet the pad of cotton once more, this time in a fluid from a tall bottle. She was pleased by her look of dewy pallor; under her wide, clear forehead, the eyebrows were sleek and dark and shining. Saints must have shown themselves like that, so innocent and candid —after a hot bath and cold cream.

It was this transparent look that she wore in the very hot days of summer. Lucia began to pat her face with the moistened cotton pad, thinking that summer was her season. Cold made her appear too frail, too wan. But in warm weather, pale and devoid of energy, she seemed to glow with a beautiful intensity of languor. Her skin was more vividly white. Her eyes seemed deeper and mistier. She never flushed, never looked unpleasantly warm. Some one had once told her that in her light, fragrant dresses, she was like a lily. That had been long ago, in that far-off other life, before she had known Jay. But it was a pretty comparison for a woman; like a lily, calm and rooted.

She was deliberately holding her mind poised in a delicate analysis, her fingers swiftly moving over her face, her hair, while she sought to quiet her foolish nervousness, her unreasonable feeling of pressure. There was plenty of time, to begin with. Jay would not want breakfast before ten o'clock. She would first go up to the nursery for a half-hour with Nickie. The car had been ordered for eleven-thirty; they were to lunch at Paula's at half-past one. With Mamma coming, with the inevitable discussions and arrangements, it might be twelve when they left the house. But Paula's household was elastic, and at a Saturday luncheon in the country other people were sure to be late. There was distinctly no hurry at all.

They were going to the Farm for the week-end, she and Jay. What could be simpler, more usual than that? The household ran smoothly. Nickie never minded their going away. They did not have to steal off secretly, like so many parents; there were never tears. Nickie accepted changes, partings, life's uncertainties with stoicism—too much stoicism, Lucia had sometimes felt, almost hurt at the untroubled lips he lifted in farewell. So, though she did not like to leave him with a new governess, still strange and unendeared, there was actually no cause for worry. Besides, Mamma would be there, and Nickie was used to Mamma—had even an affectionate tolerance for her. It could not be on his account that her fingers were uncertain as they touched her toilet bottles, stoppered, foolishly, with violets. They were not precisely trembling, the fingers; but they were not exact, there was an inaccuracy in their movements.

How absurd she was! She looked severely at her reflection. She frowned, then quickly smoothed away the wrinkle with a fingertip. Self-deception was the emptiest of frauds, no better than cheating at solitaire. For, of course, she well knew the true reason for her perturbation. She was excited over the day: May eighteenth; their tenth anniversary. With the admission, she relaxed, gave a small laugh of relief. It was useless to deny her nature; she was a confirmed sentimentalist. Perversely, against all reason, the idea of a tenth anniversary was disturbing, somehow significant.

It was, to be sure, a milestone in marriage; and

her marriage was, quite simply, the thing which filled her life. It had sometimes seemed to her that she had scarcely existed at all in the years before she had met Jay; or, at least, memories of that time appeared as familiar events in the life of another person. But actually that young Lucia Lovett— even the name was strange to her—had been another person.

They had resolved from the beginning that theirs should be a sensible marriage, the wise relation of two people who believed in freedom of thought and action. She had a natural reticence, a deeply rooted aversion to friction in her personal relationships. Jay's reserve and courtesy had admirably suited her. They had been able to make their compromises with each other's habits and ideas with a minimum of discord and inconvenience.

They were proud of being considered a very modern couple. Sometimes they made separate appointments, often they liked quite different people. If Jay dined out, she never thought of questioning him. Their relation had no place for suspicion or petty jealousies. Yet, in spite of their independence, they could plan this week-end trip to the Farm, where they had spent the first night of their marriage. They could still go away, just the two of them, on the trip they had always planned for their tenth anniversary, a sentimental expedition which their sophisticated friends laughed at.

vii

The day was fair, the sky was clean blue—how wonderful it was going to be! Ten years ago . . . it had been cloudy in the early morning; almost as though a hand had closed over her heart. But the afternoon had been fine, with a diffident fineness, sulking behind brilliant, restless clouds. When she thought of that day, the ten years slipped away like water. Impossible that it had been so long! But confronted by the bright reality of the red and blue morning glories on her bathroom walls, she admitted the amazing fact. She was a woman of thirty-two, married for a decade. Life was fuller, richer, different.

Ten years ago today . . . she had had just such another dressing case. The initials had been L. L. then; L. L. F. now. There had been fewer bottles when she packed it that time, fewer squat jars. She had been only twenty-two. She must remember to change the nightgown, the pink silk one wouldn't do.

Mamma had said: My dear little girl, I am sure I am trusting you to a good man . . . The rest had been swallowed, with Mamma's tears. She had pretended, politely, to ignore the tears—she had seen Mamma shed so many, so ludicrously many, that she had formed the habit of disregarding them— and she had concealed her resentment at the doubtful tone in which Mamma had spoken. She had disliked the choice of words: *trusting*, as though Jay had been Mamma's selection. From the moment when she met Jay—from the moment when he came into the room that first time, before they had been introduced—she would have gone with him anywhere. Actually she had felt herself rising when she saw him in the doorway, so handsome, so blond, so assured. But she had been most carefully brought up, and she had sat down again very quickly.

They had not been introduced for some time. He talked to other people, it was endless. But at last some one brought him over. She was wearing white, embroidery and lace, with a pale yellow girdle, and her hair was dark on her neck. She had looked up at him with her heart in her wide eyes, and for all her careful upbringing she had not cared in the least that he might see it there. He had said carelessly, You're coming with me, out on the lawn, to see the new moon. And she had answered, Yes.

viii

She had not been able to analyze his attraction for her. It was simply that she preferred him to other men, wanted to be with him, was impelled to do as he directed. There was in him some power, some arrogance—qualities to her meteoric and incomprehensible—which drew her inevitably. He was totally unlike the other men she had known.

Young as she was, she had been able to see that he was confident with women, but this had aroused no perversity in her, no antagonism. One day he had said to her, We're going to be married. So she had told Mamma, We're going to be married.

Mamma had cried openly at the wedding. She had worn silver gray and her sapphire necklace, and Lucia had been sorry to see her spoil the effect by reddening her nose and eyes. Mamma always had a lavender-pink blotch on her neck when she grew emotional; it combined badly with gray. All this Lucia had seen coldly, in a dizzy, obscured dream, in which the lilies-of-the-valley trembling in her fingers were a far more vivid reality than Mamma's tears. Yet always with a dreadful distinctness she could remember the little gray figure, clinging to Archie's kind, supporting arm; while Randolph stood impatiently on the other side, pretending not to notice her, a thin, handsome boy, very conscious of the flower in his buttonhole.

Ten years ago to-day, Archie had been there, darling Archie. Randolph was all right, he was clever and amusing; but Archie had been so different. Why had he had to die? It was unthinkable that he could have been blotted out in a foolish automobile accident, a crash which might have been avoided by a moment's foresight. She still had moments when she rebelled against the thought that Archie should have died like that. He was too valuable, something should have prevented his casual loss. And she thought gently of Mamma, remembering how she had depended on Archie, remembering how she had been as flattened and lifeless as a flower found between the pages of an old book.

What a life Mamma had had! She was so silly, so pretty, so helpless and extravagant. A patient man could scarcely have put up with her, and Papa had not been a patient man. They had quarreled bitterly. That was Lucia's memory of her childhood, hearing Papa and Mamma quarreling. As children, it had frightened them all terribly; even Archie had been frightened. She and Randolph had huddled close to him, because he was bigger. They had always avoided the governess at such times, because they were ashamed, because they knew it was not nice for parents to quarrel.

ix

Papa had died when Lucia was sixteen. There had been a white peace in the house after the funeral, a strange, dreadful quiet which filtered through the rooms. The children knew that he was in the cemetery, and would never come home again to storm at Mamma and make her cry all night.

He had been a man of violent nature, and he had died violently, all alone, shaving in the bathroom. His face was twisted, and Lucia had heard the doctor telling Mamma that he did not think the children should be taken to look at him. Ah, the relief of that moment when she heard that they need not look at Papa! She and Randolph had tiptoed softly past the darkened room; they had not had to go in. Archie had gone in, of course; he had had to support Mamma while she stood beside the coffin. Archie had never been spared anything.

So often had the story of their father's injustice and cruelty been poured into their young ears that the children expected nothing less than perfect happiness, after he was gone. But Mamma did not greatly change. She was older, not so brilliantly pretty as she had been. Her life must have been dull. As time went on, she appeared to grow more and more inconsolable over Papa's loss. It had much the same effect upon her that his presence had formerly had. She missed him, perhaps she even missed their quarrels. All her emotion was centered on the children; she hated to let them out of her sight, though they were happy only when they were away from home. Then, there was not so much money as there had been, for some of Papa's investments turned out badly and Mamma had never known how to manage.

Lucia had been very glad to marry, and get away from Mamma. After a childhood filled with emotional conflict, it was wonderful to live with Jay, to find that he was reasonable, ready to discuss situations and problems sanely.

In the last few years, since Archie's death, Mamma had gradually grown gentler, less complaining and rebellious. She was a little broken, a little old, though she would not have admitted it for worlds. She was still sufficiently fretful. Always she would be pretty and silly and helpless and extravagant. But she had come to accept things. Her children had left her alone. She no longer tried to fasten on them, torment them, absorb them. Some passionate need for this had died in her.

Most of the happiness in Mamma's life had come into it through Jay; for, of course, she had soon grown to like him. His kindness at the time of Archie's death had won her completely. Far more than Randolph, he had taken Archie's place in her life. It was Jay who advised Mamma about her little investments, her small holdings of property. She turned to him in every difficulty of her fussy existence; he was always ready to listen to the most trivial and tiresome story. And he paid her pretty compliments, praised her shoes and dresses, rallied her on hypothetical admirers. He made her a generous allowance, in addition to large gifts at Christmas and on her birthday.

Oh, Jay has been so good, Lucia thought, so more than kind . . . She rose abruptly and went into her bedroom.

x

Rachel stood before the shelves of the cupboard, sorting a filmy pile of underwear, freshly laundered and ribboned. "Good morning, Mrs. Fanning," she said seriously. "Did you rest well?" She was an elderly woman, with well-brushed gray hair and large, capable hands. Lucia admired her. It definitely added to the pleasure of her day to hear Rachel's ceremonious, invariable greeting; and she always answered a little vaguely, "Yes, thank you, Rachel. Quite well." She went to stand beside Rachel at the cupboard, selecting two garments of fine linen and wide lace.

"I'd like some mineral water, please. And plenty of cracked ice. No, I'm not ill," she explained. "Just thirsty. And I want my yellow négligé, the new one."

"Won't you have a cup of tea in bed, Mrs. Fanning?"

"No, I'm breakfasting downstairs this morning. Just the mineral water." Actually, she thought, the water in the bottle by her bed would have done just as well, or nearly as well—well enough. But she wanted to give instructions, to please herself by having something done for her. "Plenty of ice, please, Rachel," she said again.

The maid hesitated a moment, then crossed the room to Lucia's dressing table. "I think you didn't see these, Mrs. Fanning," she said. She held up two small satin boxes. "Mr. Fanning gave them to me last night. He said to leave them where you would see them this morning."

Lucia took the boxes, she held them in her hands.

Some hesitancy, almost tinged with apprehension, made her slow to open them. She set them on the edge of her dressing table, and seated herself, and at last she lifted one of the soft lids. Within was a pale, threaded confusion of gems which, as Lucia drew it forth, proved to be a bracelet—delicate lozenges of pearls, caught between frosty bands of fine diamonds. The other box contained a second bracelet, an exact duplicate of the first. For a moment she let them lie clustered, each in a bright, starry heap, in the palms of her hands. Then she fastened them on her wrists, sliding the slender diamond clasps. She sat with her wrists limply, almost stupidly, outstretched, as a little dog sits when begging. The delicacy of the bracelets entranced her. She patted them gently with her finger-tips. It made her happy that she liked them so much. They suited her utterly, and Jay's gifts had not always done that. In the leather jewel box on the dressing table lay her engagement ring which she had worn to the party the night before, because she felt that she sometimes ought to wear it when she went out with Jay, so that he would not be suspicious of her explanations that she was afraid of losing it or that it was too heavy for her finger or too large to wear under a glove. She remembered the moment when Jay had given it to her, slipped it proudly on her slim finger; she had scarcely recognized her hand with the great gem on it. It was so large that she had thought of it, not as a diamond—that was a

word too usual and unimpressive—but as a frag-
ment of mineral, a pure and colorless piece of crystallized carbon.

Rachel came back, stepping so softly that the
chink of the ice was the only warning of her presence. She filled a tall glass with the sparkling
water.

"I'd like to offer you my congratulations, Mrs.
Fanning," she told Lucia formally. "I hope all your
happiness may continue. Mr. Randolph is downstairs," she went on. "He said he has come for
breakfast."

Lucia drew a stocking slowly over one foot. "Has
Charles given him breakfast?" she asked. "I suppose Mr. Fanning won't be up for another half-
hour."

But Randolph, it appeared, had expressed a wish
to wait. "He has been at the telephone. He is in
the library now," Rachel told her.

"Well—" Lucia shrugged her shoulders. Let
him wait, then. He had said nothing last night about
coming over for breakfast. She had planned to
begin the day alone with Jay. It was so like Randolph to invite himself to join them on their anniversary morning, without so much as a telephone call
in advance.

Randolph never thought of any one but himself;
the way he acted toward Mamma proved that. He
refused to live with her; he had a studio apartment
with Adrian Morris. Lucia found it hard to forgive

Randolph his abominable selfishness. Her breath came short, she felt almost ill when she thought of his living in a studio apartment with Adrian Morris.

Naturally, it was all right, she would be glad to have Randolph for breakfast. But he consulted no one's convenience but his own. This morning it suited him to come to a family breakfast, so here he was. But he couldn't live in an apartment with poor Mamma; that was out of the question for him. And why didn't he have to be at work this morning?

There was no reason why she should put herself out for Randolph. Naturally she was fond of him; he was her brother. But now her plans were made, she was going up to the nursery to talk to Nickie. She was not even going to stop to call down to Randolph: "Hello" or "Nice of you to run over" or "Have a good time last night?" She put on her négligé so swiftly that all its pale yellow and ivory draperies were with difficulty arranged. But at last they were in order; the yellow draperies properly submerged, the ivory draperies triumphant, the lace smooth and level across her breast.

xi

Quickly she ran up the stairs. She looked in the playroom, but Nickie was not in the playroom. The door which led to his bedroom stood open and, glancing in, she saw him sitting up in bed, very straight, in his small white night-drawers.

"Nickie," she cried. "My darling, you're ill!"
She flew across the room, yet by an effort she kept
herself quiet, in order not to excite him. "Lie back,
sweetheart. Why didn't some one tell me?" She
sank on the side of the bed, her hand darting to his
forehead and the thin, sweet back of his neck. His
skin was cool and moist and, relieved to find it so,
she kept her hand on his face, stroking it tenderly.
As she touched him, love shone in her; she had
come radiantly to life. She gave out tenderness, as
a shaded lamp gives out light; it was like a pearly,
warm glow softly diffused about her. Yet she saw
her hand on his brow, the cool, capable mother-hand
—white and firm, with fine lines etched on the
knuckles and slender, burnished nails.

"Hello," said Nickie. He spoke gently, in-
gratiatingly. It was unmistakably an evasion.

"You've been naughty," said Lucia. "Miss Fiebiger is punishing you!"

Nickie looked absently across the room. "See
that boat," he remarked. "I made that yesterday
in school."

But she tried to look at him coldly. Her face
was sad, for it had given her such a fright to see him
in bed; and she could not bear having him naughty,
she could not bear having him punished.

"What did you do?"

He saw that he was trapped, and he began his
recital frankly, even with a shade of pleasure. "I
said I wouldn't eat my oatmeal. There were specks

in the cream. It was horrid oatmeal. *She* said I
had to eat it. She tried to make me. Then I called
her a bad name. Shall I tell you——?"

"No, never mind the name," Lucia said. "That
was very, very wrong of you, Nickie. You make
me unhappy when you do things like that. You will
have to tell Miss Fiebiger you are sorry."

"All right," said Nickie obligingly. "I don't like
her," he went on. "She isn't pretty. She is like a
chipmunk. Couldn't we send her away? She isn't
pretty like you, Mother Dear."

He saw her smile, her spasm of laughter, before
she could suppress it. He sank against his pillow,
and smiled at her naughtily, triumphantly; it was
clear that he knew he had conquered her, wheedled
her back into loving him. Lucia shook her head.
She turned away, so that he could not see her face.
A bad, bad boy! But it was impossible to pretend
that she was seriously disturbed. He was her son,
her boy who loved her, who thought that she was
pretty. People would say that he was a naughty
child, yet indeed his only fault lay in the fact that
his years were few, and bigger, stronger people could
tyrannize over him and force upon him their likes
and dislikes. He was not different from older male
children. In his aversion to ugly women, Nickie
was his father's son. And, smiling to herself, Lucia
pictured Jay, forced to eat oatmeal by a woman like
a chipmunk. Oh, it would have been a very bad
name indeed, if it had been Jay!

"She's like a chipmunk," said Nickie again. He chuckled at his own wit. "Like the pictures of Johnny Chipmunk," and he pointed a small steady finger at the bookcase. Lucia, involuntarily following the finger, saw that it was pointing to a book, the book which had large colored pictures of Johnny Chipmunk's adventures.

She folded the small, outstretched hand in her own, and laid it down on the bed with an admonitory pat. Don't point, she thought to herself; those were the things that mothers should say. But a larger issue was involved, and half-heartedly she murmured, "I don't want to hear any more, Nickie. Please don't be rude."

"May I get up now?" he asked her. "May I, Mother? Mother, may I?"

"I don't know what to say," she told him. "I'll have to speak to Miss Fiebiger." She went into the hall, knowing very well that she intended, once Miss Fiebiger's dignity had been salved, to have Nickie go out immediately. The governess was coming up the stairs, and her face was very red. Lucia clearly saw how much she did look like a chipmunk. It was perfect, the little finicking, huffy mouth, the long rodent teeth. How keen of Nickie to have thought of it! Perhaps it meant that he was going to be clever like Randolph, perhaps he would be a writer. Still, of course, it was very naughty to say such things. He might even have mentioned the comparison to Miss Fiebiger. Possibly, thought Lucia, chilling a little, that was connected with the bad name. It might be that the poor thing would think of it every morning as she combed her thin, chipmunk-colored hair—every morning for all the rest of her dreary governess's life.

"I'm very sorry," Lucia began, "terribly sorry, Miss Fiebiger, that Nickie should have been rude to you. He has told me all about it. He wants to apologize."

Miss Fiebiger bridled. She was breathing fast, in little gusts which fanned her lower lip, behind her prominent ridge of upper teeth. "Nicholas is very wilful," she said. It was evident that she did not regard his conduct as an educational problem, but rather as a personal affront. "I assure you, Mrs. Fanning, his behavior this morning has been very wilful. I felt that it was my duty to punish him."

"I think you were quite right. Now when he has told you he's sorry, will you please dress him quickly? I don't want him to be late for the concert."

"You want him to go to the concert?" Miss Fiebiger's light eyebrows went up very high, incredibly high, Lucia thought, watching them go. "I would have supposed, Mrs. Fanning, that he should stay in bed for the entire morning. You will pardon me but I have had a wide experience with children— some of them very undisciplined children, too—and I have always found that a short punishment, followed by a treat, has less than no effect. If I am to act as Nicholas' governess, I must really be given the authority for a certain amount of discipline. I really must, Mrs. Fanning."

"Oh, yes, indeed," Lucia murmured. "I quite understand." She had taken a dislike to Miss Fiebiger; certainly she would never do for Nickie. But it was impossible to point that out this morning, so she spoke soothingly, persuasively. "I quite understand your point. But the concert—that is scarcely a treat. Nickie cares nothing about the concert, he grows quite restless. I have always felt it unwise to let discipline interfere with anything educational, don't you agree?"

"Well, from that point of view—" Miss Fiebiger hesitated, her pale eyes wavered. She was vanquished.

"Then the day is so fine, Nickie must not stay indoors. Why not take him to the park for an hour afterward? Now, if you'll just come in," said Lucia, giving her no time. "Nickie, get out of bed at once and tell Miss Fiebiger you are sorry."

Nickie scrambled to the floor and very straight, very virtuous, he delivered his apology. Surely he must enjoy apologizing, Lucia thought, he did it with so much grace. And her eyes turned to Miss Fiebiger. She must be touched! But her face was as huffy and ungracious as ever.

"I will stay here while Nickie dresses," Lucia told her; and she sent Miss Fiebiger off to make ready for the concert. She drew her boy to her, and put her hands on his body, a shade too slender. Nickie was not a rugged boy. Hers had been a difficult labor, and they had thought of sacrificing the baby. She had always been sure that the instruments had hurt him. He had a weak heart; though now he seemed to be outgrowing it, she lived in perpetual fear that he might sicken. She pressed her cheek against his hair, feeling love for him go out from her, like a physical emanation. Oh, my darling baby, she wanted to cry, I want you so, need you so. But she resisted the impulse, pretending to spank him playfully, so that he wriggled and laughed. I am like Mamma, she thought, trying to use my child as an outlet for my emotions; but I never shall do anything so cowardly, so cruel, she told herself firmly. And she whispered to Nickie that he must be very good while she was away, and not give any trouble to Miss Fiebiger and Grandmamma.

"I want to wear my blue suit," said Nickie. "My blue suit, my blue suit," he demanded boisterously.

"Well, here *is* your blue suit," Lucia said, "I've never heard so much noise." And, frowning and laughing at him, she watched him put it on, watched him fasten the buttons with small clumsy fingers. I could have been submerged by my love for him, she thought; I could have been all mother, fussy, nervous, careworn. That would have wrecked my marriage. Fortunately I realized that in time.

"See my bracelets," she said suddenly, and she held out her wrists to Nickie. "They are new. Father gave them to me."

He glanced cursorily at them. "He promised he would give me a motor boat," he said. "D' you suppose he's forgotten?"

"No, I'm sure he hasn't forgotten. We won't tell Father about this morning. He would be angry with you, Nickie. And I don't want him worried to-day. We're going to have a holiday, Father and I. We're going up to the Farm to spend Sunday, all alone together." She went to the closet, took down his rough little coat and hat. Of course, he couldn't understand. Yet she wished that she might make him; she could not resist telling him more. "Father and I were married ten years ago to-day. We went up to the Farm, it wasn't Uncle Revel's then; it belonged to Father's uncle. I cooked Father's din-ner——"

"Ten years ago," said Nickie doubtfully. "I wasn't here?"

"No, dear."

"Where was I, then?"

"I don't know," said Lucia. "You just weren't. There wasn't any you. Here, quick, sweetheart, put your arm through."

Miss Fiebiger was in the doorway, her face mournful under her stiff felt hat, which was sur-rounded with plump, stuffy breasts of birds, tightly veiled so that their feathers should not blow. Lucia kissed her boy, she felt his arms press tightly about her neck.

"Cheer up, Miss Fiebiger!" she cried. She could not help laughing. Miss Fiebiger looked so funny, with her stiff hat, and her hands tightly pressed over a brown leather purse. She would lead Nickie off to the children's concert, as though he were a little prisoner. She had been highly recommended as a governess, but she was actually nothing but a chipmunk, depressed and tyrannical.

xii

Lucia stepped lightly down the stairs. The door of Jay's room was open; and she saw that he stood in the hallway looking up at her, his eyelids drawn as though the light, the strain of looking up, hurt his eyes. In that moment he appeared to her very clearly, almost as clearly as though he had been, not her husband, but a stranger.

Even in his dressing gown, even though he was jaded and worn, he gave out confidence and energy. Lucia, looking at him out of the moment's isolation, saw that there was something Roman in Jay's appearance—one of the emperors, past his first youth, no longer slim. His ruddy golden hair was neatly, smartly brushed. He was clean-shaven, soaped and scrubbed. His whole face was unevenly suffused with color, and deep lines sagged under his eyes.

Yet, even in his. fatigue, he dominated the narrow space of the hallway by his heavy magnificence of physique, by his arrogant bearing, the lift of his chin.

Unconsciously, she had paused to scrutinize him. Now, starting forward, she related herself to this heavy, tired man—the heart and center of her life, the father of her son. "Dearest," she cried, "just ten years ago this morning—" But, interrupting herself, she went to him beautifully, the long, light draperies floating from her lifted arms.

CHAPTER II

i

RANDOLPH stood by a window in the library, against a claret-colored curtain; he looked Spanish, and a little like a monkey. He was thin and well-groomed in his dark suit; the tie, the socks, the triangle of handkerchief were perfect. He was a man whom many people thought handsome. There was distinction in the set of his narrow head which had, inevitably, the dent of a mastoid operation behind one ear.

"Well, Ran," Lucia said. She greeted him with a smile, a sister's smile, ever so faintly ironic—more than half abstracted, as she turned to lift and spread the lilies-of-the-valley in twin squat crystal jars. "We're seeing you early to-day. How does it happen you're not working?"

He laughed and it was a pleasant laugh, rather high, like an amused whinny. "That's a nice greeting. Can't I have a holiday? Can't I come to see my sister on her anniversary? And congratulations, by the way." He kissed her cheek. "Aren't you glad to have such an attentive, affectionate brother?"

"Of course, I am. How silly." For a moment

she rested her hand on his arm, sensible of the chink
in the armor of her irritation. For it was easy to
be charmed by Randolph, once he was before you.
That was why he was so spoiled, that was why he
could be, in everything that was of importance, so
completely selfish.

ii

Though it seemed incredible, now that Randolph
was twenty-six and a person of some prestige in his
family's eyes, there had been a time when they had
almost despaired of him. Lucia still remembered
with displeasure a certain ring of Randolph's, an
African toe ring of lumpy silver, which he had worn
on his little finger. At eighteen, Randolph had
suddenly gone very bad. Before that he had been
merely an impertinent, good-tempered boy, rather
too fussy about his personal belongings, rather too
conceited about his good looks and his cleverness
and his talent for sketching. The ring had been a
symbol of change, and it had occasioned much distress. Lucia had protested; Mamma, of course, had
wept. But their arguments had failed to impress
Randolph who was, they were forced to realize, en-
tering upon an important phase of self-expression.
He was bent on leading his own life, and keeping
others from hampering his ego in its development.
Soon he began writing verse and, what was much
worse, showing it to people.

Randolph was never disagreeable. He was merely oblivious to interference. Mamma cried and complained and made any number of scenes, without affecting his plans. He wore his toe ring and wrote his verses; littered the house with sketches, and made friends with extraordinary people of eccentric appearance and habits. Such of these people as Mamma could not endure to have him bring home, he arranged to meet outside. It did not seem to matter to him.

When a profession was insisted on, he chose architecture, and they had been relieved that the selection was so respectable. It had, however, developed that architecture meant going to study in Paris; and eventually Mamma, in the new bitterness of Archie's loss, was left alone. During his four years' absence, he had written home the most amusing letters. He was having a splendid time. He went to London, he was invited to stay at Cannes; and returning travelers brought back agreeable reports of him. Still, on his return, Mamma and Lucia, apprehensively waiting on the pier, had fortified themselves to greet a long-haired, a possibly bearded Randolph, with flowing tie and velveteen cap. But he had turned out to be very elegant and well-dressed. The toe ring had vanished. He had distinguished himself in his studies. The verses had been published, between decorative boards, by an English house. He had formed a wide acquaintance among interesting people.

It was immediately clear that, so far as the discharge of his filial duties was concerned, he was irretrievably lost to Mamma. He was very nice to her, and went to dine with her now and then in a friendly way. He sent her flowers and tickets to theaters and concerts. But live with her he would not. He accepted a position in the office of a well-known architect, and proceeded to enjoy the benefits of his manifest popularity. People liked him because he was young and good-looking, because he had ingratiating manners, and could do a little of everything quite well. Before long, Lucia was forced to accept this new view of Randolph. The decorative boards which bore his name lay conspicuously on a library table, and she frequently said: "That? Oh, it's just the English edition of my brother's verse. Some charming things. They've been brought out here—but the English do these things so well, don't they?"

In short, Randolph had turned into a definite social asset. The studio which he shared with Adrian Morris was a gathering place for entertaining people of all sorts; the idiosyncrasies of his friends no longer seemed contemptible, but distinctive or brilliant or amusingly scandalous, according to their character.

Randolph's chief value to Jay and Lucia lay in this contact with interesting people, with what is known as a Group. They had, to be sure, other groups of their own—the groups they had respec-

tively been born into, Jay's business associates and
their wives, Lucia's school friends and their husbands. These they had gradually assembled in a
loosely stitched social patchwork. But the import-
· ant and glamorous people were Randolph's friends.
The others were, in the main, cut from the same
pattern; they were well-born and well-bred and
well-off, and their views and prejudices were unfail-
ingly the views and prejudices appropriate to their
background and their position.

The Group was very different; its activities made
good conversational material at conventional dinner-
parties. Sometimes Jay introduced the subject by
saying, "We're going slumming to-morrow night" or
"We're booked for a party with those barbarians."
Or occasionally, to flatter his companions of the
moment, he added, "It's good now and then to dine
with people who know how to use a knife and fork."
Then he would introduce some celebrated name,
whose owner, it might be understood, was more
artistically than socially accomplished.

But this was Jay's little joke. Actually, for all
his defensive jibing, he thought the Group remarkable. And remarkable it was. Randolph's friends
had won recognition in the seven arts, and in many
specialized little artistic by-paths. These were, for
the most part, the well-washed and soundly pros-
perous traders in the arts. Some were better paid
than others; these had imposing apartments and

summer estates and long low motor cars. Many had only a comfortable competence. But of the grimy and idealistic and defeated few, there were almost none. Occasionally, one or two would slip in at a party; but as a rule, they maintained a lofty separation, finding justification for their poverty in the magnificence of their ideals.

Most of the members of the Group had not been bred in the same traditions as Jay and Lucia, did not belong to the same clubs, and in moments of stress were sometimes found to be lacking in the same taboos. But they were unexpected, ingenious and clever. They had in course of time accepted Jay and Lucia as people to be included in their larger parties, and sometimes in the more intimate and esoteric gatherings which constitute real acceptance into any social set.

Lucia had been the first to attract the attention of Randolph's friends. Quite a number of the men had, from time to time, fallen in love with her in a casual, indefinite manner, which expressed itself mainly in talk, flowers and dinner-parties, a few dedications and sonnets, and a great many tickets to the opening performances of plays. They had far more time for pleasant attentions than the other men Lucia knew; and, tactfully elusive, she liked having them for luncheon and tea, and for summer week-ends in the country.

Presently they had taken a fancy to Jay. It became rather a vogue to be on good terms with him,

and he was naïvely delighted at finding himself a
favorite among persons so different from himself.
Hailing him as "the financier" and "the magnate,"
they cultivated his acquaintance, the men as well as
the women, and professed to be vastly amused at
knowing this strange creature from another world.
He invested money in the magazines they started,
and the plays they wrote and produced. He bought
their pictures and their books. And in return they
dined and drank sumptuously at his table, and made
merry at parties where they encountered the fine
world and enjoyed pleasurable sensations on dis-
covering the limitations of persons possessed of
more money, position and social experience than
their own.

Recently, Jay's brother and his wife, Revel and
Paula Fanning, had attached themselves to the
Group; or rather Paula had attached herself and
Revel had acquiesced. They were already estab-
lished at their country house on the Sound, and
Paula had planned a number of elaborate week-end
festivities for the summer.

iii

"Where are you going for the week-end?" Lucia
asked. "To Paula's?"

"Yes. I told you that last night. But you were
so preoccupied with Adrian. I hear he is going

to do your portrait, in that gold lace thing with long sleeves. I couldn't bear hearing him run on about it. Not after a night like last night. Not about my own sister. That's why I came over here. He would have been unbearable at breakfast."

"Randolph, how absurd you are." She smiled, her foot moving restlessly, as she watched him fitting a cigarette into a fresh paper holder. "Where can Jay be? I want my coffee frightfully. See, Ran, if you can hurry him."

Randolph leapt agreeably up the stairs, and Lucia went down to the dining room. "We'll be ready at once, Charles," she said. Rosy lights gleamed on the old polished wood of the table, where Charles was setting the pale, ice-green slices of chilled melon. She could hear Jay and Randolph, as they loitered, talking, on the stairs. She clasped her hands tightly, her nervousness made her feel almost ill. She thought that she would like to send Charles to tell them to come down at once; or, better still, she might call, "Jay. Please. Can't that wait till after breakfast?" But she could not have made her voice pleasant, it would have been plaintive and aggrieved in spite of her.

At last they came, unmindful that she was impatient, absorbed in their conversation. How glad she was that she had not called to them! The dining room was busy and important at once. Charles came with the fat-bellied urn from which a special, subdued fragrance of coffee was distilled, mingled with the odor of heated silver. Softly, with an impassive and expert care, he set it on the tray. Silver touched silver with a bright click, the sound that went with the special fragrance. There was a crisp smell of toast; and, finally, the sharp pungency of bacon, as Charles set a covered dish on the heater on the side-table.

Jay said: "Oh, my dear, you shouldn't have waited for your coffee." He took his place, abstractedly pinching the knot of his tie. It was of printed silk, a fine design of black and red on a lemon-colored ground; a gayer tie than he habitually wore. Lucia looked at it curiously, over the coffee urn. When she had bought the tie, she had felt doubtful if he would like it, but she saw that he pinched it familiarly, accepting it as a part of him; and indeed it lent a becoming air of summer frivolity to the sober gray of his suit, which was perfectly tailored over his handsome, heavy shoulders; steel-smooth in the accurate, ironed seams.

Their spoons slit the sweet, cold melon. Jay took up a newspaper, turned it quickly to the financial page, his fingers nervously pulling an imaginary moustache.

"I take it you're not going to the office?" said Randolph.

"No. A holiday. Our anniversary." He inclined his head to Lucia. His eyes went back to the col-

umns of figures beside his plate. After a moment
he pushed the newspaper away.

Randolph was telling him, "Adrian is going to do
Lucia's portrait. It seems that he asked her last
night, and she graciously gave her consent. I am
quite surprised at my little mouse of a sister. That
is how Adrian always begins his conquests: Won't
you come to my studio, and all the rest of it. Still,
I am bound to admit that such portraits as are completed show the ladies very happy, very blooming
and contented." Randolph smiled wickedly; he
said to Lucia, "Very well, I approve. I give my
consent to your flirting with Adrian. It doesn't do
to let Jay feel too sure of you."

"No man should ever be so unwise as to feel sure
of a beautiful woman." Ah, there was Jay! And,
over the coffee urn, while she filled the cups, Lucia
bowed to him elaborately, and he bowed gravely
back, as they had been doing for ten years, whenever he paid her compliments. She had always re-
joiced in Jay's admiration of her, in the fact that
he never lost an opportunity of telling her that she
was lovely and charming and intelligent.

No man should ever be so unwise as to feel sure
of a beautiful woman. Lucia's eyes were bright.
Her hands moved quickly, gracefully, among the
cups, and every motion seemed lovelier and more
important, because she saw herself clearly as the
wife who, even after many years, is still beautiful
in her husband's eyes.

iv

Randolph continued to talk. "He has been seized with a really frantic wish to paint her. It appears to be a kind of disease with him. If I had not restrained him, he would be here now, painting you at breakfast, Lucia. With coffee on your chin. No, there isn't really, that is just my humorous way. He says he could never do justice to your smile. He says it is the smile of an Italian gentlewoman of the Fifteenth Century——"

"Randolph, you idiot, will you be still?" Charles, the dish of kidneys outstretched, started back in surprise. And Lucia tried not to laugh, tried to pretend that it was all nonsense, and most displeasing to her. "It's too ridiculous, the words you put into Adrian's mouth. Well, even if he did say it, it's absurd. It's one of those remarks which appear so clever and mean nothing. Italian gentlewomen of the Fifteenth Century smiled like every one else. Various smiles." But the fingers with which she swept back the draperies from her arms were swift and triumphant, the confident fingers of a woman whose world is secure.

She sipped her coffee, feeling her life weave about her with a rhythm of fulfillment and co-ordination. Now, vaguely, she was satisfied, content, as sometimes even the most imaginative and intelligent people are content for a brief moment, touching an island of peace between unrest and disillusionment.

She realized this dimly, in some under-consciousness, which murmured ironically, How simple you are. Compliments and hot coffee! . . . Yet the irony was powerless to disturb her; it was as if her brain had been drugged, and the faint voice of self-analysis could not pierce the sweet lethargy. All things were golden to Lucia; and, in a blissful haze, she saw Charles, that skillful servant, holding out the dish of kidneys to Jay. It was a fine piece of silver, massive, English—Georgian. That was luxury; having the dish valuable out of all proportion to its utility; having it heavy beyond the demands of the weight of kidneys, frail, shrunken viscera garnished with shreds of bacon. It was luxury that it should be old and English; a specialized luxury for the eye and for the imagination. And, in like manner, everything in her surroundings expressed a similar redundancy—nothing being designed merely to fill the needs of subsistence and comfort.

This superabundance she loved. Ten years of luxurious living had accustomed her to it. Yet, if Jay were to lose his money—she had often thought of that, and she thought of it now, weighing it as an incredibly remote happening against the preponderant reality of her buoyant mood—she would be forced to accept a new manner of living. She knew that she would never complain, never utter a word of regret. She would adapt herself to a simpler, a less easeful existence, sharing his ill fortune, as she had shared the prerogatives of his prosperity. She was his wife. His gain must always be her gain, his loss her loss. Now she gazed at him, breathing in the dear habit of him, the permanent, secure usualness of his fair, well-brushed hair, his heavy dark neck with the trim line of the low white silk collar which buttoned so neatly, so inevitably, on either side of his tie. And gratitude flowed from her, gratitude for his wide shoulders and strong arms and skillful hands and cunning brain, all active for her defense, her protection.

v

"Every morning," Randolph was saying, "as the cold water touches my face, I say: *Ça va mieux!* Out loud, just like that: *Ça va mieux!* I caught it from a Frenchman I had a place with for a while, in Paris. I can see him, shaking off the water, like a great dog. You know? It's become a habit with me." He paused to insert a cigarette in a fresh paper holder. "I adore habits," he said. "They have all the reassurance of ritual." And he bit a corner of toast to give them time to savor his phrase.

But Lucia refused to savor it. "What time did you go home last night?" she asked him carelessly.

"Not long after you. About three o'clock. Emmy left early, you know, and I came back. I took Mrs. Ennes home, the fascinating creature. May I have some coffee, please?"

"Who," said his sister, "was or is *Mr*. Ennes?"

She held a square of sugar poised over Randolph's cup, her eyebrows raised.

Randolph shrugged. "One of the things one doesn't ask, I suppose. Sackett East first brought her around. Perhaps he could tell you. All I was able to learn is that she spent several years in China. The rest is—mystery."

"Amazing, isn't it?" Lucia said. She smiled with one side of her mouth, her eyes contemplative. "These women, so many of them, completely without roots, you know. Cut flowers, Jay once called them. No one knows from what they have come, and one supposes there must be a reason. I don't mean all this for Mrs. Ennes," she amended. "She seems, from what I've seen of her, a gently bred person. But she must have been unfortunate, she hasn't a contented face."

"I suppose," said Randolph, "that she's been a naughty girl. Oh, a very naughty girl. She couldn't have led a serene and conventional life, not with that disturbing mouth. She has an extraordinary quality, you feel it at once—at least, a man feels it at once. It isn't just passion, it's something more meteoric, destructive. She couldn't barter, I mean, couldn't bargain and compromise with life—as most of us do——"

"As all of us must," said Jay abruptly. Out of his silence, he spoke so suddenly, so emphatically, that the others looked at him in surprise. But he smiled at once, he touched nervous fingers to his face, saying lightly, "It sounds very serious. What will Emmy say to all this?"

"Ah, don't misunderstand me. Naughty is just my conjecture. She showed not the faintest inclination to be naughty with me. Otherwise, I should be bound by my Anglo-Saxon code of honor. As she rebuffed me, I am free to speculate. The fact is, she had very little to say to me at all. She was in a terribly emotional state. She admitted that she had had a shock—a blow of some sort—from some one dearer than a casual friend, it was evident. I tried to find out who he was—but with no success."

"What an unworthy curiosity!" Lucia's tone held a faint acidity.

Randolph smiled and shrugged; addressed his brother-in-law. "You don't say anything about the fascinating Hallie."

"Oh, yes," Lucia said. "Why *are* you so quiet? I thought you admired Mrs. Ennes."

"I do admire her, my dear." He raised his eyebrows, speaking with indifference. "She is a most attractive woman. A beautiful woman."

"Beautiful is not exactly the word I would use," said Randolph critically. But, interrupting himself, he turned to Lucia. "The oddest thing; in the taxi she took out her cigarette case—I was trying to think where I'd seen one like it before. Of course, it's that one of yours with the picture on the lid, the one you bought in Rome. Wasn't it a coincidence, precisely the same picture?"

"Why, yes," said Lucia. "That very elegant flirtation. A wasp-waisted lady coquetting with her fan." She had not thought of that cigarette case for some time. It was an old snuff-box, thin and rectangular, of silver-gilt, the lid adorned in delicate and faded colors; probably French, they thought, though she had found it near the Spanish Steps. Every one had spoken of it, and for a long time she had carried it almost constantly. "I wonder where that case is?" she said. "It is so lovely, I must use it again." But, as she spoke, she remembered that Jay had long since borrowed it to carry with his dinner clothes. It was an odd cigarette case for a man, but he liked it because it was very light. He had laughingly said that he did not have to be careful; no one was likely to suspect him of being effeminate.

Charles was passing the toast, and Jay paused to take a piece. After the instant's hesitation, he said to Lucia, "That was your case, my dear. I had it with me last night, and Mrs. Ennes took a fancy to it. She asked me to let her use it for the evening."

"I'm sorry, I'm sorry." Randolph sank his head between his hands. He groaned. "I'm usually more tactful."

And Lucia looked at her brother, she held her head very high and looked at him along her nose, in a way she had, a vague, impersonal stare, as if she were looking at an empty and unimpressive dining room chair. She wanted to speak sharply to Randolph, to tell him not to talk nonsense. She could hear her voice, raised to reprove him. But with an effort she kept silence, for her self-control seemed suddenly a bridge too frail to support indignation. It would mean a self-betrayal of some sort, and presently she spoke softly, in a casual. rather affected voice.

"Every one likes that case. I wonder I have kept it so long. It arouses the lowest instincts in those who see it. I should have warned you, my dear." And, resting her elbows on the table, she touched the bracelets on her wrists, and slowly, abstractedly, she raised her coffee cup.

Jay looked up deprecatingly, almost as if surprised that she had taken the trouble to continue such a trivial topic. "It's nothing, naturally. Stupid of me to be careless with your things. I'll get it for you at once, the first of the week."

vi

How deftly, how facilely, with what oiled adjustment of excellent manners she and Jay could dispose of a situation! They respected that quality in each other. For a situation had been created, silly and meaningless though it was. All of her powers had been concentrated on smoothing that crumpled mo‥ ment, on concealing perturbation or even surprise. She was now free to examine her disturbance and the cause of it. She was breathing quickly, lightly. But why? Mrs. Ennes was one of a large number

of women whom Jay admired. At the party of the
night before, he had danced and talked with her,
and they had gone into the garden for a time. But
even if he were having a mild flirtation with her, it
was nothing out of the ordinary.

Yet through some nicety of rarefied perception,
she was convinced—she could scarcely have explained the basis of her conviction, but its certainty
seemed unassailable—that Jay had been startled by
the wish she had expressed to use her cigarette case
again; for the fleetest instant he had been thrown
off-guard. He had been grateful for the natural little
delay of taking a piece of toast, and looking at his
plate Lucia was not surprised to see that the toast
was untouched. The revealment of a brief confusion was an unusual slip for Jay, so perfectly dis-
ciplined, so skilled in social subtleties. To Lucia,
instinctively aware of the psychological importance
of the slightest observations, it argued some emotional connection with the cigarette case. It seemed
probable, then, that he had not told Mrs. Ennes that
it was her, Lucia's, case. Perhaps he had not
thought of the fact himself. He had bought the case
as a gift to her—and she saw the bright street, the
flowers on the Spanish Steps; she saw the dark little
shop—then later he had appropriated it for his own
use. Now he had unthinkingly given it to another
woman. He would have to ask her to return it, and
a reluctance to do so might partly account for his
moment of hesitation.

So Lucia concluded. In spite of the fact that she had not used the case for several months, she now felt an unreasoning desire for it. She remembered how every one had admired it, and how well it had suited various dresses. Her inclination was to say: Really, J⌐y, I don't lend you my cigarette case in order that you may present it to another woman. But that, she knew, would be wrong; she would be unable to keep a note of sarcasm from her voice, and the word *present* would be offensive, for if she did not mean to be disagreeable she would use the shorter word *give*. And, speculating on why we use long and formal words when we are displeased, Lucia dismissed her irritation and determined to put the matter out of her thoughts.

"More coffee, Randolph? I suppose that Emmy is going to Paula's, too?" she said. She was relieved to hear the round, full tones of her voice, from which the strain had completely vanished. Emmy Acker was a young actress to whom Randolph was paying conspicuous attention, and in mentioning her Lucia had a pleasurable feeling of carrying an attack into his camp. "I don't think she is looking well, really. Can it be your fault? I cannot quite determine what your intentions are toward Emmy, though I am often asked."

There, she thought, there is one for you, my dear brother. And she allowed Charles to take the coffee cup, into which she had poured just a trifle too much cream.

"Jay," she went on, looking up from a scrutiny of her finger-nails, "did you telephone the office? Is everything all right?"

"Quite all right. Miss Waring can handle anything that comes up."

"Then we can surely leave at half-past eleven," Lucia said. "Of course, I promised Paula, but I never feel sure about you. I am all ready, I have only to talk to Mamma. She should be here any minute now——"

"Good God!" cried Randolph. He dropped his cigarette, he pushed back his chair from the table. "Good God! Didn't I tell you?"

Lucia looked at her brother with exaggerated dignity. "Tell me what?" she demanded out of a suppressed irritation, a premonition of certain unpleasantness.

"I'm sorry," said Randolph abjectly. "I'm the most absent-minded fool in the world. Mamma can't come. She has a throat. She telephoned you just after I got here. I told her I'd have you call her up——"

"It's a nice time to let me know." Lucia spoke quietly, almost inattentively, as though she were preoccupied with something else. For a moment she was without thought, drawing a charmed circle about herself and refusing to admit disturbance. She rose slowly and went to the telephone and called Mamma's number. As she waited, a need of drastic action welled up in her. She wanted to exclaim passionately that now their trip, their beautiful day, was spoiled, for she could not go away and leave Nickie. But she fought the emotion back, refusing to let herself be carried away by the perversity which springs from frustration, and which forces its victim to further and more painful frustrations. Over the telephone came Mamma's plaintive voice, thick because her throat was bad; and Lucia felt her flare of emotion subside. It seemed absurdly disproportionate in its violence, yet it must have been inspired by anger at Mamma for having disappointed her. And for entrusting a message to Randolph. And for having been delivered of such a son as Randolph, if it came to that.

"Hello, hello," Mamma was saying. "Is that you, Lucia? I *knew* yesterday when I didn't wear my rubbers— Yes, it's quite bad. Very much inflamed. No, I feel all right otherwise. Lucia, why were you so long in calling me up? I have been so distressed. I knew you wouldn't want to leave Nickie with the new governess. I telephoned your Aunt Geraldine, I hope I have done the right thing. Oh dear, I knew yesterday when I didn't wear my rubbers——"

Unreasonably, before Lucia's eyes, danced Mamma's little feet, trim little feet of which she was very vain and for which she bought many shoes, setting them up on footstools so that people might notice them. They went winking, quick and perversely rubberless, through the rain. Now, of course, she couldn't come near Nickie, who was susceptible to throats.

"I know you're disappointed." There was a tearful note in Mamma's voice. "These things always happen to me. Oh dear, I don't know what I've done that things should always go wrong." And Lucia forced herself to think of other things than the perverse little feet stepping over puddles. She remembered how sweet Mamma sometimes was, like an old sachet, faded and mustily fragrant. She had a broken prettiness, like the reflection of a lovely face in a dim, faulty mirror. And, reassuring Mamma affectionately—but she did behave so foolishly, she was actually such a child!—Lucia thought about the hats she wore, hats made of hundreds of violets, in that strange cone shape peculiar to hats made of violets. They dated Mamma, the hats. She had been very pretty, very much admired when such hats were the fashion; and it was possible to see that, when she wore them, the aroma of that time floated back to her and made her faintly happy.

So Lucia was able to speak warmly and sympathetically to Mamma, in order to console her and escape from her. She repressed her irritation, for she must not take it out on Mamma. It was too unfair and, besides, Mamma had ways of repaying such treatment. "Rachel," she said, as she met the maid in the hall. "My mother is not well, Miss Fanning will spend to-night here instead. If she telephones, tell her I am expecting her."

vii

She went into the dining room. She shrugged her shoulders, and her tones held a thin irony. "It can't be helped. Mamma has telephoned Aunt Geraldine to come in her place. Aunt Geraldine is at least not worse than having no one at all." She looked at Jay and her nostrils widened slightly, for it was his Aunt Geraldine. And, as is usual when women look and speak in this way, the two men gave no answer. Lucia stood for a moment, beating back the waves of her irritation. Always in such moments the woman longs for the male to be voluble, vociferous, excited, for she has spoken to create an impression and to arouse an emphatic response. Lucia was outraged by the masculine attitude of silence, recognizing that it implied a desire to smooth things over—a refusal to feed the flame, a reluctance to throw their words, poor innocent martyrs, to ravening lions.

Out of the silence Randolph spoke suavely. "Have you any kirsch?"

"Yes," Lucia informed him. "Charles, Mr. Lovett would like some kirsch." She spoke crisply and casually, as always when she felt that Randolph was showing off.

"You're not going to drink kirsch now?" Jay asked.

Randolph laid his hand on the squat bottle which Charles had placed before him. He filled the delicate bud of the glass, set like a primrose on its long stem. "Kirsch is for all hours," he said. "A glass taken after breakfast poetizes the day." Raising the glass to the light, he squinted at it appraisingly. And Lucia turned away; she was unwilling to let Randolph think she was observing this ridiculous performance. She laid her hand on Jay's cheek, moved it over his hair, which she smoothed familiarly, with a caressing, wifely gesture. Her front teeth just touched, she spoke through them with an acid sweetness, making little rhythmic pauses before the verbs.

"Jay darling," she said, "I presume you realize that I didn't lend you my cigarette case so that you could present it to another woman?"

CHAPTER III

i

"SOME one wishes to speak to you on the telephone, Mr. Fanning." Rachel stood at Jay's shoulder, her tone discreetly tinged with regret that she must cause an interruption, require Mr. Fanning to leave his place at the breakfast table, where he still sat, jerking his finger constantly against his cigarette, so that fine particles of ash scattered like dust across his plate.

Lucia, coming from the pantry where she had been briefly examining the hampers, looked after his departing back. "Jay always likes to use the library telephone," she said to Randolph, hearing the softened heaviness of her husband's tread on the stairs. "His things are there—pencils, memorandum pads—" Her words drifted into a sigh. She fingered the unused crystal ashtray beside Jay's plate; irresolutely she scraped with her finger-nail a trace of candle-wax on the rosy brown wood of the table. Then Randolph rose, and she followed him into the hall. Charles gave him his hat of dove-gray felt; he inspected it critically, deepening the crease in the crown.

"Surely," said Randolph, balancing the hat on his

finger, "surely this is all a malicious lie, circulated by some woman who has been victimized by Jay's charms—this rumor I hear that you're going off to the Farm on a second honeymoon? I think I once read about that in a book. I never suspected that such a sentimental performance would rear its ugly head in my own family. Not cooking your dinner? Not canoeing on the lake afterward? Lucia, say it isn't true!"

He looked at his sister with such extravagantly imploring eyes that, in spite of herself, she laughed. "Of course, it's true. You may be as cynical as you like. Some day you'll understand. Or perhaps you never will. I don't know. Perhaps you haven't the capacity for loving deeply. What woman bought that tie for you? It is quite terrible. I think, I am almost sure, that those are daisies in it. Yes, they are pale blue daisies. Really——"

"How nervous you are," he said. "Why are you twisting that piece of chiffon? See, you have wrinkled it." He took the long scarf of her sleeve from her fingers and smoothed it, looking at her with a frown between his brows. "After all, it's a good thing you are going to the country for the week-end. And next week you open the Long Island house. You do too much in town, your winter has been very full."

She might tell him that she did not need advice, Lucia thought; but, finding no way of saying this inoffensively, she was silent. Randolph straightened his shoulders. He moved away, as though he could read her impatience to have him go.

"I am late," he said abruptly. "I must be getting on. I'll see you later." He turned to the door, clapping his dove-gray felt on the side of his head.

ii

Lucia, as she mounted the stairs, could hear the low murmur of Jay's voice in the library, and she went into the living room in order to avoid disturbing him. But almost at once he joined her. For an instant, he paused at the door, then he came swiftly to confront her, taking both her hands in his.

"You didn't sleep last night," she murmured, seeing the tired lines about his eyes.

"Yes, I did. As well as usual. I'm all right," he assured her. She shook her head, and he said, "Really I am, Lucy. Really I am, my dear."

"Ah, you always say that," she told him.

"Now, listen, my dear," he went on, and his clasp on her fingers tightened. "I'm terribly sorry, but I shall have to go downtown, after all. I'll make it as brief as possible. I'm desperately sorry," he said hurriedly, "to upset your plans—our plans——"

"Why, my dearest, *of course*, it's all right." She raised his hands with an impulsive movement, and pressed them against her breast. She scarcely perceived her disappointment, in her relief that she had been given this opportunity to prove herself reasonable and helpful. "You don't have to explain," she said eagerly. "How can you help it if unforeseen things come up? I am sure it's more irritating for you than for me."

"I'll be back just as soon as I can," he declared. He started for the door; but he came back as though drawn to her by some invisible wire. "You're looking especially lovely this morning, you know. I'm glad you like the bracelets." He touched them lightly, almost awkwardly, with his fingers. "They suit you." He turned her hand, palm upward, and kissed it.

Lucia stood where he had left her, closing her fingers gently over the palm Jay had kissed, as though to guard and retain the caress. It was a familiar gesture of affection with him. The habit of years had robbed it of keen emotional significance, yet this morning it stirred her afresh. The beating of her heart had quickened. She had not expected Jay to come back to her, to kiss her hand. Unable to lose him yet, she ran into the hall and leaned over the stairs to see him taking his hat and stick.

And she had to say something to him. "Nothing wrong at the office, is there, Jay?"

"Oh, no. Not at all. No." The remaining words, a repetition of his assurance that he would make haste, were blurred in his swift departure, the closing door flatly punctuating them.

iii

There was finality in that brief percussion. Sensing fully her disappointment, Lucia still leaned over the stair-rail, with a feeling that she had been thwarted, abandoned. And I actually believed that everything was going to be perfect, she thought with a sigh. She remembered Mamma's words: I don't know what I've done that things should always go wrong.

Her impatience rasped her. Now, of course, they would be so late. If only they could go straight to the Farm! But she had promised Paula that they would stop there. She would have to telephone, explain about the delay. Then she recalled that Jay had not specified the time of his return. Really, she did not know what to say to Paula.

Even more dreadful than these harassing little annoyances was the feeling of self-disgust with which she was filled. At the breakfast table she had shown such stupidity. She had spoken sarcastically of Aunt Geraldine, poor old Aunt Geraldine, for whom she had a lukewarm affection. And then that senseless remark about the cigarette case! As though that mattered! Somehow, Randolph's carelessness in not telling her about Mamma had been an overwhelming irritation, the last straw.

Lucia took her relationship with her husband with a deep seriousness. A desire to keep their life free of any friction, criticism or nagging was profoundly

interwoven with her love for him. Remembering the
constrained and apologetic manner in which he had
told her that he would have to go downtown, she
was filled with a bitter anger at herself. Ah, he
should be able to count on me for understanding,
she said, striking her hands against the stair-rail. I
have tried to understand, to sympathize with everything, everything. . . . Yet, just now in the library,
he had been filled with compunction because he was
obliged to delay their starting on the trip. That
was the word, compunction; his constraint, his
apology, his assurance that he would hurry—even
the kiss on her hand had been propitiatory, inspired
by the feeling that she would blame him for the
delay.

How utterly selfish I am, Lucia thought; and, her
head bowed, she started up the stairs to her room.
Even in this relation on which she had lavished
all the sentiment, all the capacity for idealiza-
tion in her nature, she could not acquit herself well.
And, trying to free herself from the weight of her
immediate self-reproach, she let her mind wander
over the years. The rewards of understanding love
had been so great that it seemed unthinkable she
could even for a moment let its clear light be
clouded. She had a memory which she cherished.
Once, several years before, they had been at a dinner
party. Among the other guests had been a woman,
with whom Jay had been having a mild flirtation,
and her husband, an older man who had the reputa-

tion of being jealous of his beautiful wife. In the course of the dinner—it was at the salad, Lucia remembered, the blurry cheese dressing was associated with her feeling of strain—some one had tactlessly commented on having recently seen Jay and this woman in the lobby of a hotel. The husband was seated beside Lucia. She could feel that a change ran through him, a rigidity, an affront. And, almost mechanically, without thinking, she had said very naturally, with a little laugh, that she had been late for her tea appointment, and that Jay had kindly gone ahead to carry the message. Even as she spoke, she realized how convincing her impromptu lie sounded. The conversation swept on, and the incident was forgotten.

But Jay had not forgotten. That night he had come into her room, and taken her in his arms. My dear, you have never failed me, he had said. . . . That was all; and that was everything. If she closed her eyes, and kept her mind quite still and empty, she could still catch the quality of his voice when he said those words, which had moved her more deeply than any words she had ever heard.

iv

Seeing the housemaid enter Jay's room, she paused in the doorway. Her eyes fell on the tousled bed, the tormented pillow, the spilled heap of cigarette stubs. In spite of his protestations, it was evident that Jay had not slept. And we came home so late, she thought. No wonder he seemed quiet and nervous at breakfast. No wonder he looks so tired this morning. . . . She was disturbed, for Jay, under pressure of anxiety or strain, was subject to a damaging insomnia. Only two years before, this had been an acute symptom of a nervous crisis which had eventually forced a protracted rest. What hideous nights those had been! Yet, at the same time, there had been a sweetness about caring for him; he had been dependent on her, like a child. She had made him hot drinks, smoothed his bed, read to him for long hours.

For the last weeks, he had seemed to be suffering from some preoccupation which had caused her vague alarms. He was, she knew, in the habit of speculating heavily. Sometimes she thought of the stock market as a stormy sea where her home, her lovely possessions, her very happiness and security tossed perilously in the fluctuations of values. She would have questioned Jay, but she disliked annoying him, being fearful that he might think her importunate or interfering; and only occasionally did he volunteer information about his financial situation.

But now anxiety pierced her sharply. Had she carried her reserve too far? It might be that Jay was desperately worried over some business matter, and out of consideration was keeping it from her.

He might be reluctant to ask her to make retrenchments in their extravagant mode of living; and, remembering the haste with which he had responded to the telephoned summons, she felt convinced that her conjecture was correct. Why didn't I think of that before? she asked herself. He has been bearing this anxiety for weeks, and my reserve he might readily interpret as indifference. Yet, as his wife, I should share such worries with him. . . . She tried to remember when she had shown an interest in his business affairs. Except for the inquiry just now as he left the house—she heard her thin, casual tones: Nothing wrong at the office, is there, Jay?—she had scarcely spoken of business for months. It should be possible to bring up the subject tactfully, without seeming to pry.

After all, a tenth anniversary was a good time for taking account of herself, making new resolves for the future. As the housemaid pulled the sheets from the bed, Lucia sighed. Oh, I hope nothing unfortunate has happened, she thought.

v

She drifted across the hall; and the sight of her own room, immaculately ordered since she had left it, increased her feeling of dejection, for it seemed to hold the dying scents of the exaltation and expectancy with which she had met this day.

I am like Mamma, she said to herself. She sat

vaguely down in one of the pink-and-white chairs.
Although I can see so clearly how wrong she has always been, although everything in my nature is in
revolt against the sort of wife Mamma was, I have
qualities like hers. And she thought that, perhaps,
at the beginning Papa, too, had been propitiatory
when Mamma nagged him. . . . You're looking
lovely, Jay had said; and he had spoken about the
bracelets. Unconsciously he had been trying to remind her that she received beautiful gifts at his
hands, that her prerogatives as a wife were gener-
ously recognized. How ashamed she should be that
he felt an obscure need to remind her!

If she had been a fretful, reproachful, exigent
wife, what would have been the effect on Jay? But
she knew very well, he would never have endured it.
Especially in those first years of their marriage,
when he had been far more impatient, headstrong
and impetuous than he was now. When she had felt
hurt or disapproving—and in ten years of marriage,
she confessed there were many opportunities to feel
hurt and disapproving—she had heard Mamma's little voice whining through her own. That had very
nearly always silenced her.

But if she had not been able to discipline herself
from pride and from respect for the dignity of her
relationship with Jay, she would have done it because of Nickie. The terrors and heartaches of her
own childhood rushed back over her, as she told
herself that she could never have caused her boy

such suffering. She could never have shown him the tears, the complaints, could not have caused him that feeling of helplessness before an adult, incomprehensible grief, which had marred her own childhood; or the terror of those scenes, for which Mamma was only indirectly responsible, when Papa had been so furiously angry. They had huddled close together, hiding from the governess, she and Archie and Randolph.

She had developed an absurd childish apprehension that Papa might kill Mamma. It had grown into a fixed idea. She never dared speak of it to any one, even to Archie, never put it into words. But night after night she had wakened, trembling; crept to the door and listened, to make sure that the house was quiet, that Papa was not killing Mamma. When she grew older, she saw how ridiculous this had been. Papa was an excitable person, whose misfortune it was that he could neither put up with Mamma nor leave her. There had never been any question of physical violence. But the suffering during those long nights of her childhood had been desperate. She had acquired a horror of violence which she could never lose, a fear of seeing the smooth, formal surfaces of life torn by elemental behavior.

This horror was entwined with her deepest emotions; in a way she felt that it must limit and constrain her. But for all her clear perceptions, she could not analyze it closely; it was too intimate and painful. She acknowledged that she did not fully understand herself. All her discipline, all her reason sometimes failed her, and behind them she did not seem able to probe. Her intelligence she thought of as a guide, yet it proved frail and unreliable in penetrating the jungle of her own emotions. Here the trail was lost; again, it was choked and tangled. Sometimes when the way might have opened up, her fear of lurking dangers forced her to turn back, refuse to risk an entrance.

vi

"I've packed your toilet things, Mrs. Fanning." Rachel stood in the doorway of the bathroom. "Is there anything else?"

"I don't think so," Lucia told her. She brushed her fingers across her eyes, as though this might help to clear her thoughts. "Oh, yes, there's one thing." Grateful for the interruption, she rose and went to her cupboard. From a shelf she selected a fine linen nightgown, exquisitely hand-sewn, filmy with lace. "I'll take this, please, instead of the other, the silk one." She glanced at the nightgown which Rachel took from the dressing case and replaced on the shelf. It was pink and ornate, a Christmas gift from Paula. How Jay detested such nightgowns! He used quite a coarse term for describing them. Well, it was fortunate that she had discovered it in the dressing case, fortunate that she had remembered to change it.

Looking at the exquisitely ordered shelves, Lucia thought how feminine her room was. The decorations, the dressing table, the lamps and chairs all reflected a woman's taste; and the only trace, the only intimation of a man's presence was the second bed, the bed which every night stood formally beside her own, dressed in the taffeta coverings appropriate to daytime. For, of course, Jay had his own room, across the hall. The second bed was only a symbol, a tradition.

In the early years of her marriage, she had loved to share a room with Jay. She had at first been childishly delighted by the novelty of being intimately and casually alone with him. She had liked seeing his things scattered about: his coat over a chair, his big shoes on the floor, the ties and collars, the pipe and tobacco pouch, and the funny, practical-looking toilet articles. Such little, commonplace things had seemed curious and amusing: his brushes, the lotion he used after shaving, and an absurd combination nail-file and buttonhook of which he thought very highly. When she sought to recall the happiness of those first years, these were the things of which she thought. Her mind always veered away from the recollection of her early love relation with Jay; perhaps because the barrier of her modesty had been difficult to break down and she had been slow in becoming accustomed to the devastating intimacies of love.

Four years ago, when they had bought the house, Jay had suggested that they have separate bedrooms, and she had been conscious of a pang of disappointment. Of course, he had been right, she had admitted it at once. He had said that privacy was the first essential to a happy marriage relationship. Besides he was restless, slept badly; he was free now to turn on the light, to read and smoke for as long as he liked, without fear of disturbing her.

It was to be expected that a man nearing forty, high-strung, preoccupied by business, should not have the emotional force of a youngster. For one thing, he lacked the youngster's feeling of adventure, curiosity. This did not mean that he was in any sense an old man or that he had lost interest in women. On the contrary, he might be disposed to dissipate such emotion as he felt in light and casual associations with women. This would be especially true when he was under some strain; for example, if he were seriously worried about business matters, he would naturally welcome the novelty and distraction of a flirtation. Love-making in the restricted sense would scarcely come into his mind.

Strange, Lucia mused, that an experience which at first seemed unnatural and amazing, could become an accepted habit. A little startled by her own immodesty in definitely phrasing the thought, she confessed that she desired her husband. Or, rather, she wanted him to desire her; that she told herself, was a woman's feeling about love.

vii

She said to Rachel: "Let me have my brown suède shoes, with the buckles. And the new dress, the tannish one." And, slipping her feet into the narrow shoes with square, glittering buckles, she examined her use of "tannish," a foolish, half-hearted adjective which she disliked. Privately, she called the dress "biscuit-colored," but that seemed an affected term to use to Rachel, as any figure of speech, however homely, is more pretentious than a simple expression. So she had thought of the word "tan," which Rachel would at once understand. But she was not quite prepared to admit that the delicate pale brown of her dress could be described by the stupid banality of "tan." So she had weakened "tan" into "tannish." . . .

There is an exhilaration in the acute analysis of a mental process, however trivial. Lucia felt quite pleased with herself for having thought out the reason for her choice of an adjective. She put on the biscuit-colored dress, sheer and pale. She had not worn it before, and she turned slowly before the long mirror which was set in the door of the bathroom. There, you have been absurd, she said to herself, you attach too much importance to little things. You should try to conquer this propensity for hairsplitting, exaggeration. This sensitive conscience of yours is getting to be a nuisance. Everything will be all right, you will see. . . .

"Tan becomes you, Mrs. Fanning," said Rachel, bending to straighten the hem of the skirt. But Lucia had forgotten what color she chose to consider the dress, seeing that it suited her very well. It was excellently made; the silhouette was slim. The roundness of the neck flattered her slenderness, and from the shoulders flared a graceful little cape. She looked very elegant, very modish. She could not resist getting her small hat of wood-brown felt, and trying its effect with the dress.

From her jewel-case she took a long necklace of tiny pearls which she wound about her throat until they fell in a fine clustered profusion. Jay is very good to me, he gives me beautiful presents, she said to herself. Why had she thought of that? The pearls were pretty but, after all, if it had not been for the new bracelets—of course, she must wear those to-day!—she would have liked to appear without any adornment; perfectly simple, perfectly chaste. It would have confused Paula, who was always imitating her. Lucia toyed with the idea of confusing Paula. But guiltily recalling that she had not telephoned her, she instructed Rachel to call Mrs. Revel Fanning's country house.

How irritated Paula would be! Lucia wished that she had asked Jay to have his secretary call her from the office. Yes, that would have been far more sensible. Paula would not question an official, impersonal message of that sort. And, moreover, she, Lucia, had no knowledge of Jay's plans, of the hour at which he now intended to start.

"Wait a minute, Rachel," she said. Yes, that was the thing to do. She would telephone Jay; if he was too busy to speak, she could talk to Miss Waring. It seemed to her that in this way she would gratify her obscure desire to bring her husband close to her for a moment; and, if he spoke very lightly and cheerfully, it would relieve her, she would know that all her anxiety had been caused by her overactive imagination.

She felt eager now; her vagueness and depression had vanished. As she waited for the answer, she saw the spacious, marble-pillared halls of the trust company, she saw the shining brass gratings and the neat clerks, all so much of a pattern. Impatiently signaling the operator, she let her mind play over the great financial institution of which Jay was a part. She often thought about it; but always imaginatively, fantastically, instead of in the practical way which Jay would understand. She thought that privilege was a substance from which great structures are cut and reared; that money, in a thick, golden stream, ran sinuously, invisibly, through those halls, between the marble pillars, past the neat, unamazed clerks. . . .

Mr. Fanning, a girl's voice informed Lucia, was not in the office that morning.

"Let me speak to his secretary," Lucia said in a superior tone. But Miss Waring was equally firm.

"He telephoned me earlier, Mrs. Fanning. I told him it would not be necessary to come down. I understood you were leaving town———"

"But it's later I mean, Miss Waring. Half an hour ago there was a call for him. Don't you know anything about it?" But, as she spoke, it occurred to Lucia that Jay had not mentioned the office. She had simply taken it for granted that he was going there.

"I'm sorry, I must have been out at the moment," Miss Waring said hastily. "I'm afraid I couldn't trace the call for you just now."

"Have you no idea where he might be, who might have telephoned him?" Lucia asked; and her tone was a little cold, for she felt that Miss Waring might be exercising her famous discretion.

"I'm sorry, Mrs. Fanning. I haven't. I'm sorry I can't help you."

Lucia replaced the receiver on its hook with an exaggerated deliberateness. Wasn't that just the sort of secretary that men admired! A conscientious spinster, inelastic of mind and body. Naturally she was not expected to tell every one where Jay might be; but in talking to his wife, she should be free to speculate a little. She, Lucia, was intelligent enough not to call him up if he were in an important conference; it would have been comforting, somehow, to learn about him, even indirectly.

Now she would have to telephone Paula at once; and, suppressing a sigh, Lucia again requested Rachel to call the number. She tried on the light silk coat that matched her dress, thinking how she disliked the necessity for answering Paula vaguely, evasively. Paula always knew all about Revel's plans. Yes, thought Lucia, naturally she knows, because she makes them for him.

viii

Paula's gushing, vivacious tones came jerkily over the wire, the emphasis heavy on certain words.

"It's too dreadful! Lucia, I'm just *provoked* at Jay. . . . Nasty old business! Oh, dear! It was going to be so nice. Sackett East is here already. And Penelope and Eva and heaps of people will be here for lunch. Oh, and that old beau of yours, Lucia. Luis French. He broke a week-end date *especially* to see you. . . . Well, of course, you've simply got to stop in after lunch, you can see him then. But I told him *lunch* and now— . . . I can't bear having my party spoiled. . . . Yes, it is, too, spoiled. You and Jay were the guests of honor. I declare, people are going to think there's something queer, the way you and Jay avoid us. . . . Well, then, come the first minute you can. . . . I don't suppose you can help it. But, really, Lucia, on your *anniversary,* I think Jay *might* stay away from the office for *once* . . ."

Lucia sank back in her chair. Exhausted! There was the only word to describe her state. What a woman, what a sister-in-law! Revel, she should think, would be worn to shreds. She rose, and, ex-pelling a long breath with an audible *Oh,* she pow-dered her nose and arranged her hat and hair. This was how Paula, in concentrated doses, always af-fected her. Yet she was on excellent terms with her sister-in-law; not even Jay was aware how much antipathy she felt for Paula. Certainly not Jay! She had always concealed her feeling from him, for there had been a time when he had admired Paula very much. That phase, Lucia was thankful to recall, had been of short duration.

Aunt Geraldine was reported to be waiting below, and Lucia instructed the servant to send her up. So Paula had captured Luis French for the week-end. For some reason the idea amused her, teased her lips into a small ironic smile. She laid out her purse and gloves; she was entirely ready to go and, ab-surdly, it made the waiting more endurable. She was going to be very nice, most especially nice, to poor Aunt Geraldine. She rose to greet her.

ix

Aunt Geraldine, Jay's Aunt Geraldine, put out one lean cheek, and with a soft plop of her lips she kissed the air an inch or two away from Lucia's face. This meager old lady had been a devoted

mother to Jay and Revel. She had gone to her
brother's house at the time of his young wife's death,
and when a few years later he, too, had died, the
responsibility for his sons had fallen on her. In
her modest, bewildered manner, it might be read
that she had been sustained by no sense of her own
virtue.

Lucia took her arm and pressed her into a chair,
smiling upon her with conscious benevolence. "Sit
down, Aunt Geraldine. It's so good of you to
come." But her attention was fixed on Aunt Geraldine's large, deep mouth, which she always opened
hesitantly for a moment before speaking. Cavern-
ous, with long, uneven teeth, it reminded Lucia of
the muzzle of an old dog. Might she bark? Lucia
wondered vaguely. How odd it would be if Aunt
Geraldine should bark! "I appreciate your coming
so much," she said.

"My dear Lucia, I am always most happy to help
you out in any way I can." The voice, slightly
nasal, altogether meek, came surprisingly from such
a mouth. Aunt Geraldine raised her handkerchief
to her nose, looping it limply around that organ
while she produced a duplicate liquid sound, apologetic in character. Ah, she will never bark, Lucia
said to herself.

The old woman slowly peeled off one long glove
of brown silk. She had dressed in brown as a girl,
and so she continued to dress. Her hair was brown
and her faded eyes, and even her lips and skin had

a pale brown tint. Lucia was startled to see how little difference the removal of the glove had made. She had thought at first that those were Aunt Geraldine's arms, and she looked for reassurance at the arm on which a glove still remained. Brown and wrinkled, crapy from washing, it was scarcely distinguishable from the other arm, the bare one.

"Let me take your hat and fur," the younger woman suddenly exclaimed, as though eager to demonstrate some affectionate concern. "And what a pretty hat, Aunt Geraldine! It's a new one, isn't it? *Very* smart!" She turned it admiringly in her hand, before laying it on the bed. "Jay and I are going away for the week-end," she went on, and by her lifted eyebrows, by a coaxing graciousness of manner, she seemed to imply that their plans were almost dependent for their enjoyment on Aunt Geraldine's approbation. "I suppose Mamma told you? Jay's been so tired. It will be a change. We were going to stop at Paula's for lunch," and she gave a little account of their plan and its frustration. "Jay is terribly busy," she ended, sighing. "I'm afraid he's working much too hard." In spite of her efforts to sustain a cheerful manner, the corners of her mouth drooped.

"Oh dear," said Jay's aunt. Her tongue made a deprecatory noise on the roof of her mouth.

"So I'm especially anxious not to give up our week-end, you see," Lucia more brightly continued. "Yet I wouldn't like leaving Nickie alone with the governess. I don't know what we'd have done without you to help us out, Aunt Geraldine. On such short notice, too! Just between ourselves"—she lowered her voice, making a confidante of the older woman—"this new governess isn't going to do. I've said nothing to her as yet. But she's not the right person for Nickie."

"Is it," Aunt Geraldine asked timidly, "that she does not appear competent?" She wore an air of distress at the idea of incompetence, as though she might be obscurely to blame.

"Perhaps she's a little too competent." Lucia paused, bit her lip, as though wondering how she could explain a statement so anomalous. "Nickie, you know, is often difficult to manage. But I don't want his spirit broken by too much discipline. Oh, it's so easy to make important issues out of nothing, to multiply rules and penalties until a child is quite miserable. I won't have that! I'm not expecting perfection in a governess. But for Nickie she must be some one with patience and humor. A sense of proportion. Sympathy for a child."

She had said the right thing, for Aunt Geraldine looked pleased and eager. "My dear Lucia, I am glad to hear you say that. It was the same with Jay. Nickie is very much like Jay." She sat stiffly forward in the comfortable chair; a light had come into her drab brown eyes. It was evident that this simple fact, that Nickie should be like Jay, was to her a miracle, something intimate and beautiful and kindling.

"I wish Jay realized that," Lucia said. "He is very strict with him. It's traditional that bad boys turn into stern fathers. I must warn Nickie about that." And she laughed at her own idea, foreseeing the flood of questions which she would bring upon herself if she warned Nickie. But, catching the stricken look in Aunt Geraldine's eyes, she hastily said, "Of course, Jay is devoted to Nickie. They're the greatest friends. It's simply that he is more of a disciplinarian than I am."

Aunt Geraldine looked down at her wrinkled hands; clearly she was not quite satisfied. "I would not say that Jay was a *bad* boy," she objected diffidently. "He was very self-willed. He had so much strength of character. Have you ever noticed, Lucia, that the good children are usually those who have not much strength of character, who are not going to amount to much later on?" The old woman twisted her gloves between her fingers, almost animated as she thought of the days when she had had the responsibility for two boys, when she had been needed and busy and important. "The things Jay used to do! You wouldn't believe me, if I told you. You know, he used to go out a great deal with a friend of his father's—a Mr. Morton, you never knew him, Lucia, he died some years ago. Gall stones, very sad, he left very little—" Aunt Geraldine's eyes held a hunted, bewildered look, as she perceived how she was being helplessly drawn away from the subject of Jay. "Well, what was I saying? After Jay's father died, Mr. Morton used to come to the house and take the two boys out driving. He owned a number of fine racing horses, and one day he happened to tell them about a horse he had bought that was surely going to win some big race, I don't remember the name now. Well, I declare. I ought to remember. Hmm. No, it's gone. Well, anyway, when Jay came home that afternoon, he begged me to give him some money to bet on the horse. Can you imagine, Lucia? A little boy, only eleven years old, wanting to bet on a horse! Of course, I told him no. Well, without my knowing it, that child went to work——"

Stealing a glance at the clock on her dressing table, Lucia allowed her attention to wander from the story. She had heard it a dozen times; how Jay had secretly gone off after school, pledging the loyal Revel to silence; how he had done errands for a grocery store, earned four dollars, bet on the horse, and won forty dollars as a result.

"You see, he got his way," said Aunt Geraldine, with a flickering smile. "The next year we sent the boys away to school. They needed a man's hand. But that wasn't the end of Mr. Jay by any means. He was always mixed up in something, it seemed to be his nature. Fights and breaking rules, getting himself hurt in football games——" Aunt

Geraldine actually broke into a stifled, shame-faced laugh. "Lucia, he was as wild as a hawk."

"Yes," Lucia said. "Yes, of course. He was as wild as a hawk when I married him. What ignorant fools young girls are! At least, I was. Jay swept me off my feet. If I reasoned at all, I thought that he had good manners; he was deferential and charming with me. I didn't question any further." Her eyes were very still, and she drummed lightly with the finger-nails of one hand on the glass which topped her dressing table. "Of course, he's settled down now," she added with an effect of carelessness; and, addressing one finger-tip to the disposition of the hair at her temples, she looked at her reflection in the mirror. "He doesn't do wild things any more. Or, at least, not when I am with him. What he may be doing when I'm not there, I've naturally no idea." On this, with a final twist of the finger, she relinquished her inspection, and turned to Aunt Geraldine, with a small smile which left one corner of her mouth almost undisturbed.

In the old woman's throat, something moved, tightened. "Lucia," she faintly cried, "you don't mean——"

The younger woman raised her eyebrows. "No, of course, I don't mean anything," she protested lightly. She tossed her head with a small impatient movement, as though the scene held for her something almost unbearably annoying. In her former speech her voice had had a quality of brittle re-

straint. Now, suddenly, rising to her feet as though
to break the spell, she spoke quite naturally, with
all her gracious, pretty urbanity. "It's selfish of
me to keep you talking here! I'm very thoughtless,
Aunt Geraldine. You must want to go to your room,
leave your things. Go right up now, won't you?
Wouldn't that be best? I'm putting you in the
Maple Room. Rachel will see that you have everything you need."

Aunt Geraldine's face wore a funny, baffled expression. She obediently crept to her feet, she took
her hat and fur from Lucia's bed, and began moving slowly toward the door. But "Lucia!" she stam-
mered, turning jerkily; as though she had been
forced to do it, unexpectedly. "Lucia, I couldn't
bear—oh, I know I shouldn't speak of it to you, but
to hear you talking that way about Jay—" There
was pain in her voice; her fingers clutched the hat
so tightly that the feathers were pushed awry. "It's
made me so happy," she difficultly continued, "to
have him married to a woman like you. I've noticed so often how well you've managed him. My
dear, I don't speak in a spirit of criticism, you understand. So many people would have nagged him,
tried to make him do things their way. You've
shown such wisdom, Lucia." She paused, and by
the humble, puzzled look in her eyes, in which her
appeal yet hopefully fluttered, she seemed to acknowledge her own incoherence.

"Why, Aunt Geraldine!" Lucia laid her hand

on the old woman's arm. There was affection in her tone, and regret. She made no pretense of misunderstanding; gave at once her gentlest, most sympathetic smile; so that again, as in the nursery, a soft glow seemed for a moment to emanate warmly from her. "You couldn't suppose that I meant to criticize Jay seriously? I was joking, my dear. It's a silly habit of mine. Please forgive me for being stupid." Putting her arm lightly around Aunt Geraldine's waist, she led her to the door. "We're the happiest people in the world! But, of course, I don't need to tell you that. I love Jay far more to-day than when I married him." On the last words her voice slightly trembled.

x

She had chosen the Maple Room for Aunt Geraldine because it was cheerful and pretty. But it was difficult to think of her among its shiny chintzes, the crisp drapings of the dressing table, the quaint china figures and gilded vases of flowers. It was almost displeasing to imagine Aunt Geraldine finding rest beneath the azure canopy of the slender four-poster bed, lying between the fine linen sheets like an old coffee stain.

Lucia shrugged her shoulders, crossing the room to her dressing table. Here she seemed to pause in a moment's indecision. Clearly she was not pleased with herself, for she compressed her lips, shaking her head with a little frown. But, as Aunt Geraldine's steps could be heard descending the stairs, she appeared to accept an abruptly formed resolve. With a quick, almost guilty gesture, she grasped her gloves and purse; she hurried to the door.

"I'm terribly sorry," she sweetly said, as she encountered Aunt Geraldine, laden with light tan wool. "I have to go out. Not for long! Just half an hour. I hate leaving you, Aunt Geraldine. You must come in for lunch next week. We haven't had a real chance to talk. What nice, soft wool that is! Not *another* sweater for Nickie! Paula's going to be very jealous. Well, that's too lovely. Now, you're sure you don't mind?"

She patted Aunt Geraldine's arm, she patted the light tan wool; and, pulling on her gloves, she ran down the stairs. Oddly, as she ran, she remembered a story she had read in a newspaper, about a man lost in a swamp, who had been driven mad by the bites of mosquitoes.

CHAPTER IV

i

TURNING without hesitation into Madison Avenue, she walked quickly northward for a few blocks. Then, rounding the corner, she approached a large house of Italianate aspect. Formerly a mansion of the brownstone-front period, it had been reconstructed with much outward embellishment of plaster and fancy ironwork. A square tile depicting a plump mermaid, was sunk in the plaster over the arched doorway. Lucia eyed it with displeasure; and, stepping into a blue-green vestibule like a little grotto, she pressed one of a row of buttons. A convulsive clicking of the latch advised her that she might enter.

The two top floors of this house were occupied by Randolph and Adrian Morris and a small, shrimp-like Japanese servant. Peering up the dark curve of the stairs, Lucia saw the servant hovering politely at the top.

"Good morning, Amado," she said. "It is Mrs. Fanning."

Amado bowed politely, backing into the open doorway of the apartment. He held the door wide, he effaced himself behind it. Lucia went into the entrance hall.

"I came to look at the samples for Mr. Lovett's bedroom curtains," she said. "Is he at home?"

But it appeared that Mr. Lovett had gone out for breakfast and had not yet returned.

"You wouldn't know anything about the samples, of course, Amado? No, I suppose not." Lucia tapped one forefinger hesitantly on her lip. "Well, I might wait for a few minutes. Is Mr. Morris in?"

As though she were sure of his answer, she had already started up the narrow stairs which led to the studio.

ii

Except for Adrian's small bedroom and bath, the studio occupied the entire top floor of the house. It was vast and light, adorned with faded crimson velvet and gold brocade. Lucia tiptoed across its shining, rug-strewn floor, feeling that impulse to quiet which a large, unoccupied room engenders.

"Who's there?" called a loud voice from the bed-room.

"It's Lucia," she said. "Surely you're not still in bed? Why didn't Amado tell me?"

"Ah, Lucia!" The voice was somewhat lowered; it expressed gratification and surprise. "Not really Lucia? Just a minute. There, now. Come in."

She went, still stepping lightly, to the door. Adrian was sitting up in bed in a dressing gown of gray watered silk. On a table beside him was a tray, littered with breakfast dishes. He looked hearty and well-fed. His red hair rose in a ruffled crest above his pink brow.

"Lucia, sweet thing!" He held out his hands for both of hers. "Forgive my receiving you like this. I'm such a lazy fool. But there's something lovely about receiving you in bed. Yes, it's very piquant. It's wonderful, it's charming!" he shouted, and laughed uproariously.

He drew his dressing gown about him, and moved to one side of the bed. "Here, sit down, sit down beside me. But, no, you look reluctant. I can see you will not be comfortable. Now nice of you to come! How did you know I would be at home?" He discovered among the bedclothes a large silver box of cigarettes, and offered it to Lucia with a sweeping gesture.

"You are always at home in the mornings," she said, dismissing the silver box with a shake of the head. "You are far too lazy to be anywhere else."

"She knows my habits!" he cried delightedly. "It is an excellent beginning." He gave her a significant look, his eyebrows raised.

"But I didn't come to see you," she told him, dismissing the look, too. "I came to see the samples for Randolph's new curtains." She paused, settling her small brown hat. "Do you think he will be back soon? He spoke of some errands. I have only a few minutes."

"You might at least pretend that you came to see me," he grumbled. He ran his fingers through his bright hair. "That's my complaint about you," he pointed out. "You are never flattering, you have no technique. But at any rate you are here, that's the main thing." On this he produced a gallant smile, which gave him a youthful look. "Now I suppose you think I should dress? It would not take me long."

She nodded. "I'll wait in the studio. Certainly, you should dress. I shall feel much more at home."

"As you wish," he said. "Some women—! Ah, well!" The long groan of his sigh followed her into the studio. He called after her, "There's my last portrait on the easel, almost completed. You must tell me how you like it. If I am so lazy, how do I get so much work done? Explain that, if you can."

iii

Adrian Morris had started his career by painting landscapes in the romantic manner, and these had won him a considerable reputation. But gradually he had become aware that all was not well with his work; that the notable painters, the young glamorous fellows were no longer doing it that way. Once this discovery had crystallized, those first smooth sentimental canvases seemed to him so much expert crewel-work. Young and keenly ambitious, he had turned his talents to portraiture. Some of his despised early pictures he destroyed, others he denied, a few of the better-known he endeavored to laugh off as youthful folly. A number, said to be hanging in the Mansard mansions of Middle Western millionaires, were buried in a safe obscurity. The report of the sophisticated was that Morris had done well to abandon those accurate sunsets, autumn scenes, snow-bound brooks and Venetian canals; that they were, in fact, rotten with verisimilitude. . . . That, thought Lucia, observing the canvas on the easel in Adrian's studio, was a charge seldom leveled against his portraits.

As a painter of portraits the fame and fortune of Adrian Morris had been brilliantly secured. His second success had eclipsed the first. To think of a Morris was to think of a portrait. Adrian's name, scrawled in the corner of a portrait, meant something in dollars and in prestige. It was a badge of social distinction to have been painted by this hand. Adrian's annual income was counted in five imposing figures.

Adrian was a success, he had a vogue, and he carried it off so beautifully. He never heeded the jibes of his critics. He was dignified even under the plaudits of his admirers. But his confidence in his work, his feeling that he was an exceptional and distinguished person, exuded persuasively from every word and gesture. It was never offensive; it was too completely convincing. As long as you were with Adrian you were persuaded that he was a great man.

On the easel before which Lucia stood was an excellent example of his work. It was a portrait of an elderly lady in evening dress, thin, elegant and indifferent. A feathered fan seemed about to fall from her tenuous fingers. Her chin was a shimmering point, and long eyelids drooped under high-arched brows. She looked like a greyhound. All the ladies in Adrian's portraits looked like greyhounds.

iv

Lucia turned as Adrian, shouting for coffee, came into the studio. He appeared vigorous and fit. Over his clothes he had slipped a dressing gown of rough silk, a faded green which set off his fiery hair. His open shirt collar revealed his strong, ruddy neck. He scrutinized the picture with an air of satisfaction, looking blandly from the easel to Lucia's face. Apparently he was waiting for commendation.

"How do you like it?" he at last was forced to ask her.

"Very much," she told him. "Oh, very much!" But she could not help laughing.

His eyes questioned her, and rather dryly, as though chafed by his self-complacency, she said: "Women come to you for reassurance, don't they?

I'm sure you never fail them. It's very delightful that you're going to do my portrait. At least, it will be flattering to see myself with that exquisitely disgusted expression about the nostrils." She pursed her lips and looked again at the portrait, her head on one side.

"You are being sarcastic," he said. "Ah, you're very sly about that sometimes, for all your sweetness. But I shall take no notice." Amado had brought coffee, and he poured himself a cup. "You are full of little poisoned darts this morning," he loudly complained. "That is always a bad sign in a woman. It means she has been frustrated. Are you frustrated, dear Lucia?"

She showed indifference to this. "Oh, very likely. But all that will be changed, once you have done my portrait. I shall be fortified by the thought of those supercilious eyelids, those elegant hips." She sat with an air of impermanence on the side of a great armchair, frowning a little and looking at her finger-nails.

"What a mood you are in!" Adrian drew a cigarette from a shagreen case, and tapped it competently on the back of his hand. "You are difficult, you are temperamental. It is very becoming. But what can have caused it? Ah, I remember. You expected to go away this morning. Is that it?"

Reluctantly she met his gaze. She assented simply, thoughtfully. "I—suppose so. I suppose I am disappointed."

"You have quarreled with Jay?" His tone was eager, but not quite serious.

"Oh, of course not." She slapped her gloves impatiently across the palm of her hand. "How absurd! Jay and I do not quarrel. It is merely a delay, we shall be starting in an hour."

Adrian rose from his chair and, bending over her, closely regarded her face. She smiled at him faintly, a trifle self-consciously. He did not at once draw away, but remained staring at her with a strange, trance-like look in his eyes. The gleam of his red mouth, the healthy texture of his skin were near her face. Some emanation of his person, at once an odor and an electricity, might have pervaded her, for she slightly averted her head. He went back to his chair.

"You have an amazing quality," he admitted, frowning. "I never realized it until last evening. Sometimes I've wondered why I never found you disturbing. You're beautiful. And there's a kind of pale fire in you, but it is so shielded, so screened —it isn't possible to get warm." He stretched out his hands, as though to a blaze, and made the gesture of withdrawing them, disappointed.

She was animated by his words. "I won't pretend to misunderstand you," she said. She left the arm of the chair, to seat herself more comfortably. "Adrian, you funny old thing, always measuring life with the same stick, don't you see that I'm happily married? Does it never occur to you that a woman can be? That, fascinating though you are, the pale fire is for some one else?" She was very much in earnest; a faint color had come into her cheeks.

Adrian struck his hands together, he opened his mouth wide. "Lucia," he shouted, "I believe you've never had a lover!"

Her lips just parted, closed, and parted again. "Of course, I haven't," she told him, with a little gasp. Her hands grasped the arms of the chair; she uncrossed her legs, and set her feet sedately beside each other. "Of course, I haven't," she said again.

"Well," said Adrian. "Well—" He smoothed his bright crest of hair. His tone, his grimace implied that he knew such things must be; he must accept them and be patient about them.

She was rather chilled and distant. "You've known too many French women," she told him.

"Maybe I've known too many American women," he retorted, his chin lifted.

"But I don't see how you could have thought——"

"I didn't think," he grumbled sulkily. "What I said was absurd. I didn't mean it. You provoke me with your nice, sheltered life, your nice, sheltered thoughts. You don't know what goes on in the world. You see only what you want to see. I get a perverse impulse to make you see, to open those gentle, blind eyes of yours. It's my native sadism," he shouted; and, having thought of this, he laughed. "I suppose you're cold," he went on, after a moment. "Pale fire. That's cold, isn't it? It is only because you are beautiful that I phrase it so prettily."

v

She rose, slowly pulling on her gloves. "I ought to be going," she murmured. "Though I can scarcely tear myself away, my dear Adrian, you are being so excessively charming."

"You're not angry with me, are you?" Looking anxiously into her face, he took one of her hands, on which the glove was half-drawn, and retained it in his own. "I did not mean to criticize you. We are as we are, as our temperaments direct. Yes, I can see you do not like my way of talking. You think I am a coarse fellow. Don't think that, Lucia."

She had a small smile for him. "I'm not angry. How absurd!"

"And I am the one who is frustrated. You know that? Lucia, you're a good enough psychologist to know that? I have been speaking bitterly out of my perversity, because you do not like me as well as I like you, since last night." He made it sound very pitiful, and he looked sadly down at her hand, turning back the glove with long, agile fingers.

"Yes," she admitted, "I know that."

He laughed to show her it was not so very important. "You're a gentle thing. Why should I wish to change you? It's never wise to wish to change any one. You like to lay yourself away in lavender. Well, that's your way. There's the very fragrance of sweet lavender about you, dear Lucia. You are like a good housekeeper's linen closet——"

She cried out, she snatched away her hand. "You are horrid! I've never been so offended! I will not be called anything so odious." She repeated the phrase with loathing. "A good housekeeper's linen closet!" She sniffed. It was done elegantly, but it was a sniff.

He was pleased to have piqued her. "Ah, that's better! Your indignation is delicious. Why must you be so calm? Why not let yourself go now and then? Emotion is becoming to you lymphatic women."

"We see life from different standpoints," she told him. But her gaze, once more serene, was friendly.

"But that need not prevent our being friends, need it—Lucy?" He breathed the name gently, almost affectionately.

"Don't call me that!" she cried, and blushed at her own vehemence. She smoothed the back of her glove. "That is a very private name. There, you may say I'm as sentimental as you please."

vi

Below them a door slammed, and a voice came sharply up the stairs. "Adrian, have you packed?"

"Of course, I've packed." Adrian's reply was prompt, but he looked guiltily at Lucia. "What do you suppose?" he indignantly shouted.

"I suppose that you have not. Go on, get ready—" Randolph's head appeared between the slats of the railing. "Lucia! I say, what in the world are you doing here?" He ran quickly to the top of the stairs.

"I'm sure I don't know." She was pleasantly vague, with a little shrug. "Adrian is being very disagreeable. I came intending to look at those samples for your curtains, but you hadn't left them for me."

"But where's Jay?"

"He had to go to the office."

"Had to do what?"

"Go down to the office. Office. Business."

"Oh."

"What did you say?"

"Nothing. I was just surprised. I thought he said he didn't have to go, that was all."

"Well, that telephone call was to say that he did have to go. I just ran over for a few minutes. I'm going back at once. What a nagging wife you would make, Randolph!"

He called down the stairs: "Emmy! Come up and defend me. Lucia says I'm a nagging wife."

A slim girl came up the stairs, and crossed the room with a dragging, affected walk. Emmy was taffy-blonde, with a pink-and-white face, flat and snub-nosed, like a Pekinese. One hand was thrust into the pocket of her green homespun suit. With the other she waved a vertical greeting which shook back the bracelets from her wrist. Emmy was the permanent, vivacious *ingénue*. She had a wide, lovely mouth; and when she smiled she wrinkled up her diminutive nose. She had acquired certain traces of an English accent, which she used lavishly on occasion; it was her company accent. Among her repertory of imitations—which she obligingly gave on the slightest insistence—were those of a Cockney girl and a London swell. She was always picking up some round object and screwing it into one eye for a monocle.

"Hallo," she said to Lucia and Adrian. "Hallo." She prolonged the second syllable, smiling and wrinkling her nose at them. "What do you think? I've the most divine new play," she announced with a childishly egotistical confidence in their interest. "For next year. It's a secret. I can't tell the name. But it's too ripping. I'm to be featured."

"How splendid!" said Adrian. "Oh, Emmy, you're so adorably simple. And how you simple people do get on!" He sighed.

She bent her supple knees in a small courtesy. "If you please, kind gentleman, don't make game of a poor girl who's only trying to earn an honest living." At the last words, her tone turned to burlesque, and she put her fingers to her cheek with a derisive gesture.

"Here, Emmy," said Randolph. He came forward, holding out a large, square, shallow box. "Why am I carrying this? Do you want to take it with you?"

"Of course. Paula asked me to bring it. It's my astrology board," she explained. She took the box from Randolph's hand, and removed the lid, exhibiting a complicated arrangement of movable colored cardboard disks, superimposed one upon another, and labeled with numbers and months and the signs of the zodiac. "I'm too fearfully psychic, didn't you know?" She jerked her small green hat rakishly over one ear. "You see, you find the date of your birth—the month and the day. Then you arrange the board so as to discover the influences, the stars, you are under at any given time. For instance, this is May. . . . You look up in the book—Ran, old bean, you haven't lost the book, have you?—and find out what your fortune is, don't you see?"

"Yes, you've explained it beautifully," Ran told her. "I wish you were a teacher, Emmy. You're wasted on the theater. You should help to unfold little minds."

"Don't laugh at me," said the girl, pouting. "It's perfectly clear. *You* understood, Mrs. Fanning, didn't you? You know, it's frightfully useful, I run my life by that board. I can tell fortunes by cards, too. I told Paula I'd do it this evening, if nothing better turned up. I can read palms, too. Cross my palm with silver, pretty gentleman."

Randolph took her slender, outstretched hand, and pressed it between his own. "Now will you excuse me for a moment?" he said. "I have a couple of things to put in my bag. Adrian, take off that dressing gown and get yourself ready. Cocktails will be up at once, I ordered them when I came in. I'm the only one with the remotest sense of appointment. We're lunching at Armand's, we can drop you on the way," he concluded, turning to his sister.

vii

"How executive Randolph is," said Lucia. "It is so seldom I see that side of his character. Really! And attention is paid to him. There goes Adrian to pack."

Emmy gave a bubbling laugh, with a little catch in it. She was shaking idly in her hand a cylindrical box, which Randolph had been carrying for her. The box gave out a dry, chattering sound.

"What's in that box?" Lucia asked.

"Those are my Chinese sticks. It's another fortune-telling thing. You see, there are bamboo sticks inside the box, all numbered. You shake them, like this, until just one stick drops out. It tells your fortune for the day. Every morning I start off with a fortune from one of these—they're quite priceless sometimes. I say, Mrs. Fanning, while we're waiting, shall I tell your fortune?"

"Very well," said Lucia. "Yes, I would rather like to know." She smiled indulgently at the girl.

Emmy shook the cylindrical box very slowly. "Mrs. Fanning, you looked too lovely last night," she said. "Did you have a fearfully good time? It was a ripping party, but I was tired; I went home early. Randolph was furious at me! But I don't see why he cared, he went back after he took me home." She tipped the box, still shaking it, and gradually several of the sticks protruded beyond the rest. "He made a pass at Hallie Ennes and she turned him down. Isn't that a marvelous joke on him? But I could have told him what would happen. Hallie was most frightfully upset. She had some sort of quarrel with your husband, didn't she? She looked so tragic, she wouldn't even say good-night to him." Emmy laughed artlessly. She shook the box so quickly that one of the sticks advanced far beyond the others. "Did you notice her that time they came in from the garden?"

"No," Lucia said. "No. I was with Adrian most of the evening. He's so absorbing, Adrian. You don't have time for other things when you're with him." The bamboo stick fell with a light slap on the table.

"Isn't Adrian jolly?" said Emmy. "I think he's the most frightful dear. Oh, I say, you've a seventeen. But—isn't that too absurd? I can't tell your fortune because Randolph has the book! We must remember the number, seventeen. Oh, and did you make a wish? Did I forget to tell you to make a wish? Well, we'll do it all over again when Ran comes up."

The servant appeared urbanely at the head of the stairs. He bore a silver tray on which were cocktail glasses, and a shaker.

"What can Randolph be doing?" Lucia suddenly exclaimed. "He never is ready, it's too annoying." She bent over the stairs, hesitating for a moment. Then she hurried down and knocked at his bedroom door. "Ran," she called, "I had no idea it was so late. You must come at once, or I'll have to go on, I shall have to take a taxi and go on."

CHAPTER V

i

Lucia leapt swiftly from the car, as Randolph drew to the curb. At once Charles opened the door.

"Mr. Fanning didn't come in yet?"

"Yes, Mrs. Fanning."

"Oh, he did?"

"You will lunch here, Mrs. Fanning?"

"Well, I suppose so. Yes, we'll have lunch at once."

Nickie was waiting for her at the head of the stairs and she took his hand, looking through the wide doorway of the library, where Jay sat talking to Aunt Geraldine. He was leaning forward, his heavy shoulders stooped, his clasped hands dropped between his knees. She could hear the patient, considerate note in his voice, as he explained something to Aunt Geraldine.

Her breath fluttered. "Oh, those stairs!" she said, and put her fingers to her throat. "You're back already, my dear."

"Yes, I hurried as quickly as I could," he told her. "I knew you wanted to get an early start. You shouldn't run upstairs," he added. He drew up a chair, and she sank into it, lifting Nickie be-side her.

"If you will stop in at the office some morning, I'll go over that with you more fully," Jay told Aunt Geraldine.

"Are you talking business?" said Lucia at random. "I should think you would be tired of business." Her arm encircled Nickie, holding him close.

"It was my fault," said Aunt Geraldine. "I asked Jay—I didn't mean——" Her hands wavered on her knees.

"Dear Aunt Geraldine, how stupid I am! I seem to say everything wrong to-day." She sighed, mov-ing her fingers which Nickie had grasped in his own: the thumb and first finger in one hand, the remaining fingers in the other. He sat very quietly, pulling her fingers. She laid her cheek on his hair, too neatly brushed. Nickie was forlorn, an unusual state of mind for him. Once he sniffed, and his small shoul-ders stirred.

"Did you like the concert?" she whispered to him. He nodded slowly. "Yes, Mother?" she suggested.

"Yes, Mother."

Charles came to announce luncheon, and they went downstairs. At the door of the dining room, she turned, looking closely into Jay's face.

"Everything all right?"

"Why, quite." He bowed gravely, his tone was light and deprecating. "Quite all right."

"I am sorry I kept you waiting. I didn't realize

you'd be back so quickly. I'm all ready," she added. "We can start as soon as you please."

"Whenever you like, my dear." He drew out her chair, and took his place. There was an indifference in his manner, the indifference of weariness. Charles whisked in the tray of *hors d'œuvres;* and, as she served herself, Lucia took two quick little looks at Jay. He seemed preoccupied, his chin thrust out, his eyebrows raised; his fingers abstractedly pinched the knot of his tie.

ii

She ate very little. At length, she sat back in her chair, Nickie's hand in one of hers, the other holding a cigarette. Jay looked at her attentively.

"Shall we go on then?"

"Aren't you going to have any more lunch?"

"I'm not hungry. If Aunt Geraldine will excuse us——"

"Jay, you've eaten almost nothing!"

"I've had quite enough. I'm really not hungry. We breakfasted so late."

"Well, then——" She rose quickly. "It's only for the week-end," she vaguely said, looking at Nickie. "Aunt Geraldine will read to you, I know," she went on as she left the room, "if you ask her nicely. And you will be good and eat your oatmeal, my darling?" She turned to Aunt Geraldine who had tentatively followed them into the hall; observing

Jay, as he told Nickie good-bye, she lightly touched that brown cheek with her lips. "Keep Nickie with you as much as you can, won't you?" she murmured. At the doorway, she held the little boy in her arms. She seemed reluctant to leave him, but Jay stood waiting. "Good-bye, sweetheart," she said, and gently freed herself from his clasp.

She followed her husband to the car, smiling back at Nickie who ran out on the sidewalk to wave after them. The motor stirred, and Lucia turned to wave to the small figure. Aunt Geraldine put out her hand to Nickie and, still watching the car, he suffered his own to be grasped. He did not look at Aunt Geraldine, but he recognized the authority of her extended palm.

iii

The clear spring air sparkled, the park was fresh and green, and from the pure sky sunlight poured over the crowds of people who walked on the sidewalks and drove in the streets. On Fifth Avenue they sped northward in the stream of traffic. Jay drove the car expertly, with a competent ease of manner which suggested indifference to risk.

Lucia scanned his profile. "Really you ate nothing for lunch," she said.

"I wasn't hungry. I ate something. Enough."

"Don't you feel well today?"

"Perfectly well."

"You look rather tired."

"Well, it was late last night when we came home."

"Didn't you sleep well?"

"Fairly well. As well as usual."

"Jay, why do you tell me that? I am quite sure you did not sleep well at all."

"Well, my dear, that should save you the effort of asking me." His tone affected humor.

"I'm sorry, I didn't mean to be annoying."

iv

Lucia caught the side of the seat, as they swerved rapidly past another car. They were leaving the city, traversing the ugly fringe of spoiled clearings with which a metropolis makes contact with the countryside. There were stark new apartment buildings, interspersed with old frame houses and occasional ruined shanties. Half undeveloped street, half desolated lane, the route was increasingly bordered by barren lots, signboards, dirty trees.

For several minutes she had been silent, evidently preoccupied with some disturbing thought.

"I didn't like to leave Nickie," she at length confessed. "I suppose that's silly of me . . ."

"Rather silly, perhaps." He was ready to dispose of this lightly. "I haven't heard you say that in years."

She defended herself. "He didn't seem happy. Didn't you notice? After all, he's only a little boy. Naturally he's sensitive to the people about him."

"You're speaking of Aunt Geraldine?"

"Certainly not! I'm speaking of Miss Fiebiger. She's not the right person for Nickie. She has no idea how to deal with a spirited, high-strung child. I could see that he'd been crying."

There was a pause before Jay answered. "He had been crying because I had a talk with him. Miss Fiebiger told me about his behavior this morning." He spoke firmly, with a note of protest. "Lucia, Nickie is growing out of hand. He does not know the meaning of obedience."

She had turned sharply to him. "What behavior this morning?"

"At breakfast he was very rude to Miss Fiebiger. Really, dear——"

"If I needed anything," she quietly interrupted, "to confirm me in letting her go, that would be enough—that she went to you about it."

"Why do you say that?" He, too, was quiet; evidently puzzled.

"Because the matter was quite settled." She explained it patiently, drearily. "She had punished him by keeping him in bed. He had apologized to her. That should have been the end of it. Surely you see that you cannot keep bringing up offenses and punishing a child for the same thing over and over again——"

He promptly acknowledged it. "Yes, I do see that. I'm sorry then that I told him——"

"Told him what?"

"Oh, that I wouldn't buy him the motor boat." He veiled his regret with a mild impatience.

"Jay, you didn't do that? After you promised him. Oh, that was unjust of you. Oh, you had no right."

v

She was clearly distressed; she clasped her hands, seeming to make an effort to speak moderately. "He will have enough disappointment later on," she cried. "It's a shame that you should teach him that experience so soon, so unnecessarily." The vehemence of her speech brought tears to her eyes, but she forced them back. "Life holds enough disappointments that we cannot avoid," she murmured, almost with bitterness. Her face wore a startled, breathless expression, as though she were surprised by her own emotion, which had sprung from ambush to assail her.

"Why, Lucia! I don't think I was as cruel as you suppose." Her emotion had surprised him, and without rancor he tried to justify himself. "It is not so unusual to discipline a child by depriving him of something he wants. I wonder if you can make a real impression without doing so."

"Ah, but that motor boat meant so much to him," she persisted. "He has spoken of it every day.

Perhaps you didn't realize. I can't think you intended to be cruel. But not to notice—things—is almost as unforgivable as deliberate cruelty. It is so selfish, so blind—" Her fingers twisted, futilely interlaced.

"Well, my dear, I've said that I was sorry." The car veered smoothly, passing a heavy truck. "Perhaps it can be arranged somehow. Though I am sure you're wrong to spoil him. You exaggerate his sensitiveness. He seemed all right when he said good-bye to me."

"He adores you," she said. "And he's never sulky."

"That's all very well. But now he's getting to the smarty age. You're the usual fond mother. He's perfect in your eyes. But he does need a firm hand. I know, I wasn't an angel myself. They sent me away to school very young. Perhaps that would be the thing for Nickie."

A full minute passed while she breathed difficultly, her lips compressed. "I suppose most people would consider me a dutiful wife," she said at last, pronouncing the word *dutiful* sharply.

He accepted the challenge. "I don't know what you mean by *dutiful*. I've never exacted——"

"Let us say then that I've been reasonable," she proposed coldly.

"Certainly you've been reasonable." He was prepared to be conciliatory. "Now look here, my dear——"

"Then, in one thing I am going to be entirely unreasonable," she said, her voice shaking. "I'll give in to you about anything, *anything*, but Nickie. You've left me the responsibility of bringing him up. Ah, yes, you have, Jay! You have nothing to do with him, you give no connected thought to his training—except to interfere now and then, arbitrarily." She paused, trying to speak with control. "That isn't fair." After another pause, she added, "I'm going to send Miss Fiebiger away on Monday. I'll take care of him myself until I can find some one suitable."

"Very well," said Jay, promptly. Presently, he went on. "You're right, of course. You do take the responsibility for Nickie. I should consult you before I interfere. It's only that—well, my dear, he's my son, too, and I love him perhaps as much as you do. I want to feel sure that we're being wise. That's all, dear, don't you understand?"

His voice was gentle, and, pressing her fingers to her throat, she seemed for a moment to find speech impossible. "Yes," she said at last, "I spoke foolishly. I don't know why. The—the mistake has been that we don't take time to talk over Nickie. We're both so busy. Actually, I can't think when we had our last talk about him. That's wrong. If we discussed it, we could arrive at something which would suit us both. Don't you think so?"

"Yes," Jay told her. "That's what we ought to do."

"I'll try to find a governess who combines firm-
ness with the other qualities that Nickie needs," she
assured him. "And I'll have a serious talk with
him. You can appeal to his reason, really you can,
Jay. I'm sure we can work it out," she added in a
pleading voice.

"I'll try to see more of him this summer," Jay
acknowledged, after a moment. "I mean to, but
I've been so busy. There are so many appointments. The days slip by. I rush in to dress for
dinner, barely say hello to him. See him at breakfast usually. But, at that, I am hurried and preoccupied. It's a shame. I'll tell you, Nickie must
learn to ride this summer. I rode with my father
when I was seven."

vi

On an even stretch of roadway, Lucia took the
cuff of Jay's overcoat in her hand, scratched at it
critically.

"What's that on your sleeve?"

"Why, I don't know. It brushes off. Face powder, perhaps."

"I wish I knew what kind, then. If it would stick
as fast to the nose."

"Well, as a matter of fact, I suppose it's the plaster on the closet wall. I've noticed it before."

"I'll have it done over in the fall." She relaxed,
leaning back and crossing her feet. "Oh, dear, there

are so many things to think of. I dread opening the house next week. Just the idea of packing, getting things settled, arranging about the servants. And interviewing governesses at the same time! I wish I had put it off another week."

"You'll feel much better once you're in the country. You always do."

"Well, yes. It's the getting there that I dread. And of course I always hate leaving you."

"Nonsense, my dear!"

"It must be lonely for you, though you won't admit it. Still, you're usually in the country four nights out of the seven. Is that what you're planning to do this summer?"

"Why, yes, I suppose so. Yes. I really hadn't given it any thought. I imagine it will come to about that."

vii

"Jay, didn't I see something in the paper about Hagerman's failing?"

"Yes. Very likely. They went into bankruptcy yesterday."

"Oh, that's too bad, isn't it?"

"You think so?"

"Why, wasn't he a friend of yours?"

"Yes. He was."

"You mean he isn't now? Why not? I thought Revel had some connection there?"

"He did have. That's just the trouble. Revel

trusted Bert Hagerman implicitly. I never would have."

"How do you mean?"

"Well, first of all, perhaps, I mean that I wouldn't trust any one implicitly."

"Jay! What a dreadful thing to say! Oh, I can't bear to hear you say things like that."

"My dear, naturally I don't mean you. I'm not talking about the people who are nearest me. I mean, in business."

"Tell me more about it. What did Bert Hagerman do to Revel?"

"Just double-crossed him, that's all. Revel's such a confiding fool. Dear, simple, honest idiot—he oughtn't to be in business. He doesn't know what it's all about. He's full of loyalty and taking people's words for things and sticking to your friends. Hagerman induced Revel to go in on a big deal with him—oh, he was in it himself, all right, at the start. Until he found there was something queer about it. Then he quietly withdrew without saying a word to Revel."

"Did he lose much money?"

"Revel? Not very much. He hasn't much to lose. Undoubtedly it seemed a lot to him."

"Then there's a sort of justice about the Hagerman failure, isn't there?"

"Well, if it pleases you to discover a divine hand in it. But there are plenty of others, just as crooked, and prospering mightily."

"What will he do now? Bert Hagerman?"

"Oh, when the thing's settled, they'll be around, I suppose, passing the hat for him."

"You won't help him out?"

"No. And neither will any of my friends."

"You mean, you'll actually try to keep people from helping him?"

"I mean that I'll have nothing to do with any friend of mine who raises a hand for Bert Hagerman. Not when they know how he treated my brother."

"What a strong feeling of family you have! I don't believe that I'd feel that way about Randolph. Well, maybe I would if some one had wronged him. But not nearly so much as you. You have a code for your clan and a code for the outlander. They're utterly different. That's amazing! Because you seem so smooth, so civilized on the surface. You're really quite primitive, dearest, underneath."

"If that's primitive, well, then, yes, I am. You shouldn't complain."

"I don't complain. It's just that—well, it shocks me sometimes, still, to hear you admit things that seem almost cruel. You overthrow all my cherished ideals, all my belief in altruism and forgiveness and fair play. It—rather fascinates me. You're so strong and sure of yourself, without compunction or regrets."

"You've never felt that in our relation?"

"No. Ah, no! Not within your family. There you're entirely different. I've heard you bitterly condemn a man for even criticizing his wife in public."

"A man who does that is unspeakable. A complete cad. Why, he's undermining the foundations of his own house. I wouldn't have him in mine."

viii

"What a perfect day this is!" Lucia said brightly, as they drove through a village street, bordered with large white houses.

"It is a fine day. Last night I wasn't sure whether we'd be able to make it. It looked overcast when we came in."

Lucia hesitated. "But, of course, we—could have gone, anyway," she said reflectively.

"Not much fun around the Farm in bad weather."

"It wasn't such fine weather the first time." She was kindled by that memory. "Well, it wasn't raining, of course, but it had been. Everything was sopping wet, the grass and the trees and bushes. And the canoe—don't you remember, Jay?"

"I do remember that the canoe hadn't been turned over. What a useless idiot Ed Pardee is! Has always been."

"I'm surprised that Revel keeps him at the Farm,"

said Lucia, after a moment. "With an energetic, capable farmer, he might make some money out of the place, as long as Paula refuses to live there."

"Oh, well, my dear, he can't let Ed go. Why, he's been there ever since we were boys."

"How sentimental you are, darling! I'm surprised. Why not just throw Ed out? He isn't one of the family."

"He's worked for my family for twenty-five years. How do you mean, throw him out? Surely, you don't seriously think——?"

She laughed tenderly, teasingly, at his puzzled face.

ix

"Was—was—oh, Jay, don't drive so fast, you terrify me! I was going to say, was everything all right at the office this morning?"

"Why, as far as I know, everything is quite all right. I've told you that a couple of times already, I think. What's in your mind?"

"I don't know. I'm foolish, I suppose. Sometimes I get worried, thinking you keep things from me—that you're anxious about, you know. For instance, that thing about Revel and Bert Hagerman, you never mentioned that. It might just as well have been something that affected you instead of Revel."

"My dear girl, we tried for awhile that farce of your being interested in my business. Let's forget it. I promise to let you know before the furniture's set out in the street."

x

"Jay! Who do you suppose is spending the week-end at Paula's?"

"Herman Meyer."

"Oh, of course. That's too easy. Some one else."

"Give up."

"Luis French."

"French? Who's that? Oh, that old beau of yours?"

"Yes? Isn't that funny? Paula has been seeing quite a lot of him this spring. She seems to like him rather well."

"I thought he was in South America."

"He has been; for years. In Bogota, I think. He must have changed."

"Do I catch a sentimental note in your voice?"

"Yes, dear. Oh, *very* tender! I was just a girl, you know."

"And he came to slide down your cellar door? Don't think that satirical tone deceives me."

"I wouldn't deceive you for the world! Of course, there's a glamor about a girlhood romance. And Luis said such beautiful things to me! I think I'd be moved by them now, if I could remember any of them. I'm curious to see him. What does a sweet boy like that turn into? I can't imagine."

"Did you ever (you've probably told me, but I don't remember) consider marrying him?"

"Well—yes. But that means nothing. A girl considers marrying every man she meets. Don't you know that? I forgot him, poor Luis, when I met you. He was away, in Montana, or somewhere. I cherished a regret that I had broken his heart. Horrid of me! Oh, he was *very* nice. He loved me from afar—so different from you—with tender looks and beautiful words and romantic silences and what I now suspect may have been dramatic attitudes. But they were highly successful at the time. I believed in them all. He had dark eyes——"

"Doesn't it spoil the picture just a little to think of him as a hanger-on of Paula's?"

"Well, you're putting it crudely."

"I think you'll find that's what happens to the sweet boys when they grow older. They turn into admirers of comfortably married ladies. Those tender looks and romantic silences are delightful for summer week-ends. I'm basing my expectation of your friend, not altogether on what you've told me—largely on my knowledge of the type that your fascinating sister-in-law attracts."

"I can't understand why you take this tone about Paula."

"I confess, my dear, I'm getting pretty tired of her. I don't say much about it, because you've al-

ways seemed to like her. Thank Heaven you do.
It would be a very uncomfortable situation if you
two didn't get on. I thought she was charming at
first. She *is* attractive. But she's such a little fool,
I don't see how Revel puts up with it. Except that
he's the kind who puts up with anything."

"I don't think she means any harm."

"Perhaps not."

"And she has a good side to her. She's been
awfully kind, when Nickie was sick—and at the
time of your breakdown."

"It's wonderful to me how you always stand up
for her."

xi

"Haven't you any news for me to-day? You
know, I depend on you to keep me informed about
life and love among these friends of ours."

"Well, let's see. I don't believe I have, really. I
had a brief chat with Adrian this morning. But I
don't remember anything—special."

"Is he as eager as ever to do your portrait?"

"Apparently. He spoke of it. It's funny, isn't
it? Of course, I'm flattered."

"I think you've made a conquest."

"Adrian's a congenital philanderer. You needn't
worry about that."

"I'm not worrying. I agree with Randolph. I
approve of your flirting with him."

"Ah, it's amusing how eager you all seem. Unfortunately, my dear, it isn't in my nature. I'm sorry. I like to oblige—but I'm such a stupidly good girl. I'm really quite happy as I am. Or would you prefer to have me like Paula?"

"You couldn't be like Paula."

"Let's see. I was trying to remember if Adrian said anything. But no, I can't think of a thing. Emmy came in later with Randolph, looking very pretty. But I'm afraid she's a little fool, rather empty-headed. An amusing chatter-box for a few minutes. But she has nothing beyond that, not enough good breeding, I suppose to atone for her lack of brains. Have you ever noticed what a compensation social experience is, if one can't have brains?"

"You expect too much of her. Why try to judge her by standards to which she doesn't pretend? She's just a pretty, high-spirited little girl, rather a good actress."

"Oh, an excellent actress, I'll agree to that. I don't know why she annoys me."

"I know why."

"Well, why?"

"Because you never like the girls that Randolph admires."

"Why, that's the silliest thing I've ever heard!"

"It's true, all the same."

"Oh, Jay, it couldn't be true. Let me think. I've liked lots of Randolph's girls."

"Name me one."

"Well, I can't just think—offhand, like that. Well, Randolph *has* rather absurd taste in women. Don't you admit that yourself? It couldn't be anything in me, Randolph and I have never been close enough for that. Don't you see, dear? We've never been close enough."

"You're pretty keen on these psychological subtleties. You'll have to work it out for yourself."

xii

"Paula will be furious."

"Why?"

"Because she was expecting us for lunch. I told you that, darling. She was very reproachful when I telephoned her."

"Oh, well. She'll recover, I imagine."

"We'll have to stay for tea, I suppose. I hate to make it so late when we get to the Farm. I'd like to have had dinner a little early and seen the sunset from the lake—the way we did——"

"Undoubtedly we'll be expected to stay for tea. We might as well make up our minds to that. What's an hour one way or the other? Who's up there, did she say?"

"Why, she mentioned Sackett and Eva. Oh, and Penelope. Adrian, of course, and Emmy and Randolph."

"Good Lord! What an assortment! Trust
Paula for that. And Herman Meyer thrown in for
good measure."

"It isn't such an assortment. They fit together
rather well. Ah, you love to wrinkle your nose at
them, Jay. But we haven't any other friends who
are half so amusing."

"What consternation you would cause if you
asked them to list their grandfathers."

"You're so thoroughly conventional—at heart,
more so than I am, do you realize that?"

"There's a deep race wisdom in conventions. Why
do you laugh?"

"I've heard you say that so often. Dearest, it's
so *funny* of you! To mention conventions is like
pressing a button—and out you come with your
deep race wisdom."

"Oh, is that so? . . . Maybe you're right, Lucy.
I overdo my respect for conventions—perhaps.
Anyway, I talk too much about it. It implies an intolerance. You see, my dear, we're so beautifully
secure."

"Secure? How—how do you mean, we're secure?"

"Why, we have money and position and the prerogatives that go with money and position. We can
pretty much pick and choose in life, go as we please,
make what friends we like. My dear, you can't
imagine the scheming, the ambitious planning, the
scrimping and saving and keeping up appearances

and fearing to make a misstep that fill some people's lives."

"Oh, yes, I see what you mean. Of course, we are *very* secure, aren't we? I never thought of it in just that way."

"Because it's so basic in your life. Because you take it for granted, like the air you breathe."

"Jay. You don't think that we might be a little— perhaps just a tiny bit *smug*?"

"Smug? What makes you think of that?"

"I don't know. So often conventional people like us—people who are established, secure, the way you just said—are called smug."

"I certainly hope we're not. It's such a mean-sounding word. It implies, I think, that you are self-satisfied in a narrow, unimaginative way. I don't believe we're like that."

"No, we really aren't, of course. You've expressed it beautifully, Jay."

xiii

"There! How's that for making good time? We're at Wayne already."

Jay perceptibly slackened his speed, as they drove into the sedate, well-groomed street of another town. Not far beyond its limits was situated the house which Revel and Paula rented for the summers. It formed part of a large estate, bordering the Sound, which the owners hoped to sell to a land development company, and the delay in consummating this project had for three seasons made the property available to the younger of the Fannings. Though the house was no longer in the best of repair and the grounds and out-buildings had been, for the most part, allowed to deteriorate, it was a pretentious place in an excellent neighborhood, and it furnished Paula with a commodious background for the house parties which she delighted to give.

In the five years of Revel's marriage, Lucia had seen much of her sister-in-law. She felt that she understood her thoroughly. Paula, to her discerning eyes, was like a small showcase, in which were clearly displayed a number of inexpensive articles, some of them pretty, all of them trivial. Speculating on the moment of their arrival, preparing herself for a suitable response to the demands of that moment, Lucia foresaw her sister-in-law's petulant greeting. *Really,* Paula would say—but she pronounced it *weally*—I thought you were *never* coming!

Paula was bird-like, her head perpetually poised aslant, her lips protruding like a soft, pouting beak. When she talked, she closed her eyes; she had never mastered the letter *R*. Her hair was a dry, lusterless ash-blonde, the hair of an inexpensive doll. But her figure was exquisite; she had lovely little legs and feet. She had a lively patter, imitative of the vivacious conversation of those she admired. Although she lacked originality, her superficial cleverness often made a good impression.

Revel's income was a fraction of his brother's, but Paula did everything with ostentation. She insisted on an expensive apartment near Park Avenue. She enjoyed the decaying grandeur of their summer quarters, because the house and grounds were far larger than those of Jay's unpretentious Long Island property. Paula copied Lucia's prettiest dresses, she copied her hats and her appointments. She had copied even her hobby of collecting Chinese carvings; jade and tourmaline and crystal were strewn on her tables, too. And occasionally Lucia had to suffer the exquisite irritation of hearing some one say, "Oh, you have some of these funny, lovely things, just like Paula!"

It was Lucia's belief that there was a kind of vulgarity in Paula which made it possible for her to get on so well. She cultivated people through flattery, through countless little favors and attentions. She quite openly invited attention from men, but she was shrewd enough to ingratiate herself with the women as well. In edging her way into the society of Randolph's friends, she had risked snubs which would have stayed a more sensitive person. Not long after her marriage she had seen the advantage of being associated with this easy-going, artistic group. They were friends of Lucia and Jay; she had determined—Lucia had seen the resolve crystallizing in her half-closed gray eyes—that they should be her friends, too. She had often unexpectedly dropped in at Lucia's house when there were guests. On the slightest acquaintance, she invited people to her parties. She was always extravagantly sweet to them, crossing her little legs and looking into their eyes. They had not seemed to resent it. In the end—for Paula was too wise to be impatient; she had been willing to be extravagantly sweet year after year—they had accepted her invitations.

Lucia was as delightful as possible with Paula, quite sisterly, almost affectionate. Yet she had never forgotten how, in the early days of Paula's marriage, she had often chosen to sit beside Jay, crossing her little legs, smiling into his eyes. Because she respected Jay's judgment and admired his taste, she had been sorry that he had smiled back at Paula, that he had for a time talked enthusiastically about Revel's charming little wife. . . .

xiv

Under the tires of the car sounded a grating noise of gravel, as they swung into a long drive. Presently they had a glimpse of the blue waters of the Sound. They passed an old barn, half-obscured by trees, and came in sight of the large, white house which sat insolently in a green patch of lawn, as though aware, without regrets, that it belonged to a bad, comfortable period.

As Jay descended more slowly to a graveled circle beside the nearer wing, a chatter of voices could be faintly heard from a remote and unseen porch. Summoned by the sound of their motor, Revel appeared at the front of the house. Paula followed him closely and, pushing him aside, ran down the steps. She wore a white silk tennis dress, and a brown and white checked silk handkerchief was tightly tied around her fair head.

"*Really,*" she called, "I thought you were *never* coming!" At the word *never*, she clapped her hands, spreading out sharp little claws of fingers with great, glittering nails. She offered them her lips, painted the color of a ripe apricot.

CHAPTER VI

i

In the fulvous light diffused by the orange awning of the side porch, the guests were assembled. Though afternoon leisure might be read in the cigarette stubs which spoiled the saucers of their scattered coffee cups, they were looking very intense. In them it might be guessed that some flame brightly burned, at their secret vitals some fox gnawed. These were folk who lived, loved and thought at fever heat. There was no peace in them.

For all that, their attitudes seemed at the moment sufficiently relaxed. They were tossed on the comfortable, orange-cushioned furniture of the porch like so many eccentric dolls. Sackett East, the playwright—easily the lion of the occasion and the object of Paula's prettiest solicitude—lay supine on a long wicker sofa, apparently unconscious of the crackle of conversation about him. Those fingers from which had flowed so many pages of sparkling dialogue, those very fingers which had tapped out the incomparable cynicisms of *Lady Minerva*— were occupied with nothing more important than the agitated stroking of pale wattles (his own). His brow was drawn, his eyes were restless and disturbed. The great man might have been in pain.

"Well, they came at last!" Paula shrilly cried. From the doorway, she produced Lucia triumphantly. There was a staccato murmur of greeting; and, as though sensing in herself some involuntary withdrawal, Lucia selected a place at the fringe of the group, beside a handsome woman who reclined carefully in a long chair.

"Dear Lucia!" this woman sighed. Her face, enlivened by keen blue eyes, was like an expensive French glove, which has been dry-cleaned; it would not have been possible precisely to say that it looked worn. But her hands, dessicated and elegant, which moved to take a cigarette from the onyx case on her wrist, gave evidence that she was no longer young.

"Well, Eva!" Lucia smiled at the older woman with all her guarded gentleness, all her urbanity. She did not actually like Eva Tailer; but it was recurrently interesting to her that she could be the author of successful sentimental novels. "It was a nice party last night," she went on. "How do you manage to look fresh? Jay, you see, has quite a weary air after so much gayety," she added brightly, as her husband came to greet Mrs. Tailer.

"Jay? How can you tell, I'd like to know? Such a ruddy, superbly poised person." For a moment, the two women looked after Jay's heavy shoulders and arrogant head. "Now with Mark it's different. After a party, Mark is saffron and shivering. A disgusting sight. Like one of those hairless dogs."

"Is Mark here?"

"Heavens, no! I should hope not. He's gone to stay with friends on Long Island. I do hope he's being unfaithful to me this week-end." Eva sighed. "He's been so irritable. You know how it is?"

"Why—oh, Eva!" Lucia broke into a little laugh, her gaze resting curiously on the other woman's face. "You're too wonderful," she said, still laughing. With an effect of casualness, she glanced about the porch until her eyes fell on Jay.

ii

Revel stood beside Jay at the end of the porch, engaging with him in an intermittent, low-voiced colloquy. Here was the recipe for Jay, with some savor, some strength omitted. Although he was the younger by two years, although he was more slender than his brother and his face was less deeply scored by lines, Revel seemed indefinably the older of the two. There was in him a patience, a slightly stoop-shouldered acquiescence which is not a part of youth. He was of those who seem to grow older by a process of drying. Already, in the full vigor of his thirty-six years, it was possible to foresee the clean, shrunken old man he would become. This was less a physical than a spiritual indication.

Jay's face was grave; he moved restless fingers over his hair. Revel was speaking quickly, ner-

vously, with lowered eyes. He wore tennis clothes—
evidently he had just changed—and his slim, mus-
cular figure showed to advantage. Such a man, in
business clothes, looks spare and meager. His collars are invariably too stiff, too high. His ties are
heavy and thick, artlessly knotted, the ties of an
honest man.

Jay laid his hand on Revel's shoulder, and the
younger man raised his eyes. In that moment it
was evident how much they resembled each other—
in their fair coloring, their hands, the eccentric
marking of the eyebrows—yet this resemblance
served chiefly to emphasize their important dispar-
ity. Beside the maskless sincerity of Revel's face,
Jay seemed more than ordinarily subtle, acute, dis-
creet, invulnerable, lacking in scruple.

Paula, perched on the railing of the porch, was
whispering to a young Jew, with a soft, good-tempered face. But her eyes were on the brothers, and
at last she caught at Revel's shirt sleeve. "What are
you two doing?" she asked impatiently. "This is a
holiday. No business allowed, positively not a *word*.
Revel, I wish you'd just run in and get the silver
box of cigarettes. You aren't paying the *slightest*
attention to your guests. And you might get a
couple more ashtrays. Please, dear! Listen. Did
you ask if anybody wants a highball? Well, of
course, some one *must*. Will you get the tray—
listen, Revel, please look straight at me and listen
carefully. I want the *tray*, the big one, with some

bottles of soda, six or eight, the decanter of whisky that's on the sideboard, that silver pail filled with ice, and plenty of glasses. That's five separate items. Can you remember?" She had ticked them off on her pointed fingers, which she now held fanwise before his face.

iii

Once more Lucia's gaze strayed about the porch and its lounging, chattering occupants. She rose and stood looking across the brief expanse of clipped lawn, past the terrace which held the tennis court, to the distant trees below, under which the grass grew high to the water's edge. Far out into the water ran the track of the rickety pier, a float moored to its extremity. In the mild spring sunshine all was still; no figure stirred. As she turned, there was the faintest frown on her brow. Her lips parted as though she had intended to ask a question. But with a change of purpose, she went quietly to the door which led to the house.

Inside it was cool and dim. The house opened spaciously on either side of a central hallway which terminated in the rear in the kitchen. Because of its pretentious size and the many guests whom Paula entertained, it was necessary to have four servants—a cook, two housemaids and the children's nurse—in addition to the general handy-man, who served also as gardener. Under his care the lawn and a few flower beds around the house were kept in order. The tennis and badminton courts and the croquet lawn were in frequent use, and the barns and bath-house and pier had been patched and repaired. For the rest, the place ran wild, with high matted grass, straggling shrubbery and weed-choked paths.

This neglect Paula was wont to explain as her predilection, her whim. "I adore it, the wildness!" she would exclaim, striking together her little hands. "After a winter in town, I'm *hungry* for it. It's too divinely soothing to one's jangled nerves. Our lives are so remote from Nature, I think. We've lost *contact*. So we keep only one gardener on purpose, I won't let Revel get another. You see, he has so much to do that he simply can't spoil my playground by making it tidy."

Such speeches would recall to Lucia's mind that the Farm, scarcely an hour's ride away on a Connecticut back-road, was sufficiently close to nature for the simplest taste. The old place was now Revel's property, having come to him several years before from his uncle, who had kept it partly out of sentiment, partly because the small lake, which he had stocked with trout, made it available as a fishing camp. Some fiction was maintained that the Farm was profitable, because of the sale of berries and other fruits; but actually the proceeds barely served to cover necessary repairs and the wages of the resident farmer. Several times each year, Revel and Jay, who retained from their boyhood a keen affection for the place, visited it on week-end fishing trips. It was scorned by Paula except as an occasional retreat for her two babies and their nurse, when an especially large inroad of guests pre-empted their quarters on the third floor of the house.

iv

Lucia went into the large living room at the right of the hall. She did not know why she had left the others, but now that she was alone she felt a vast relief. Through the windows she heard the murmur of voices, but they no longer seemed imminent and disturbing. She drew a deep breath and looked about her.

The room was long and spacious. Walls and ceiling were painted white and the impression was that of a dusky pallor, for the light was dimmed by the wide, awninged porch outside the high windows. This house derived dignity from the immense height of its ceilings and the imposing marble mantels, surmounted by heavy mirrors. It dated from the administration of Chester A. Arthur, and the furniture was hotly coated with ruby-colored plush. This Paula had concealed by means of flowered slip-covers, welted with jade green. The lofty windows were draped with glazed lengths of rose chintz, valanced, ruffled, and tied back with Victorian decorum. There were bowls of flowers, and the many small objects which Paula transported each summer from her town apartment—pretty boxes, lamps and Chinese carvings. Most of the pictures had been allowed to remain on the walls. They were, in many instances, quaintly amusing; and one or two family portraits in wide gilt frames achieved even a stiff and formalized excellence.

Lucia took off her hat and light silk coat, smoothed her hair and powdered her nose. There was running water in an alcove in the back of the hall, and here she washed her hands, drying the fingers slowly and meticulously. As she stood in the alcove, which was placed in the space under the stairs, she heard steps descending above her head. She dropped the towel hastily, and turned to the hall. But she moved quickly back, and in the mirror gave her face a bright, informing scrutiny. She moistened her lips, smiled, raising her eyebrows. She pushed with her palms at the dark bands of her hair, softening it about her face. Then she stole through the hall and glanced into the room she had just left. By the table a man stood examining a tennis racquet. His back was turned to the door. She saw that he was thin, of middle height, wearing flannel trousers and a silk shirt. The back of his neck and his forearms, which were bare, showed dark.

"Luis!" she cried, but softly, so that her voice should not be heard on the porch.

He turned at once, dropping the racquet and

stretching out both his hands. This gesture he immediately altered to a handshake almost stiffly formal, save for the long duration of its conventional pressure. He stood silently before her, his head slightly bent, gazing at her with a remembered upward look, luminous and intent.

She hastened to break the silence. "How long it's been!" she exclaimed with a little laugh; and, drawing away her hand, she moved to a small sofa. "Shall we sit here for a moment? Won't you give me a cigarette? There, in that box." She composed herself on the sofa, while he secured the cigarette and looked about for matches.

"I'm afraid I haven't any myself. I shall have to give you a light from mine," he said, taking his cigarette which smouldered on an ashtray.

"Oh, that's quite all right. Of course, that will do nicely," she assured him vivaciously, almost effusively. She put the cigarette to her lips, and he held the glowing tip of his own against it; but it slipped unsteadily, and she could not get a light until he rested the side of his hand against hers. "There, now I have it. Ah, that's better. Thank you so much," she cried, and abruptly stopped. He had seated himself at her side, and she looked at him with an effervescent expectancy, an air of delicious, experimental anticipation, like that which a young girl wears when she receives the first advances of an attractive man. It was evident in her eager, almost tremulous animation that she wanted

to talk, to laugh, to be brilliant, to be beautiful.
She smoked her cigarette quickly, constantly putting it to her lips, constantly blowing out the smoke
with a little upward puff. As though recalling that
this trick sometimes left a faint stain of nicotine on
her upper lip, she took her handkerchief and touched
the place; ran her tongue over her lip, and touched
it again.

"I'm looking at you very attentively," she told
him. "I'm trying to make out if you have changed.
Of course, you have. Naturally, in so many years!
You have a mustache, that always makes a difference. Such a funny mustache, Luis. Like a tiny
shoebrush." Her breath caught on a little gasping
laugh. "Still, I think I like it. You're thinner,"
she went on, "and ever so much darker. That's the
sun, of course, and all the years you've been working in the open. Your eyes are more romantic than
ever."

His lips just parted in a smile which showed teeth
brilliantly white in his dark face. A dozen fine
lines deepened with the movement of his mouth.

"Why are you so silent?" she asked. "Come, say
something to me, Luis. What about me? Am I so
changed?"

"You are not changed at all," he said. "You are
the same. You are—just as you were." He bowed
his head, and his eyes seemed to rest on her hand
which lay beside her on the sofa.

"Ah, that's never true! I don't think it's even desirable. Yet how we love to hear it," she said in a sad voice.

"Are you happy?" he asked her so suddenly that she was startled.

"Gloriously." His silence appeared to be a mannerism, and after a moment she went on. "More than any one has a right to be. Frighteningly happy. You know what I mean? We both had that superstition about happiness, do you remember? I have it still. I'm so happy that it's like tempting the gods. They're jealous of too much good fortune, perhaps. I try to armor myself by imagining all sorts of frightful eventualities. As though the anticipation of evil were a safeguard against it. You know?"

He nodded. "And you?" she asked. "Are you happy, too, Luis? You haven't, I think, a happy face. But perhaps it's only your nose, and you can't change that. You have one of those nervous, hawk-like faces which give an impression of secret suffering. Ah, that look, with those romantic eyes of yours, should have served you well with women."

"It has," he assured her, with a sour smile; and, his head still bowed, he again fixed her with an upward glance of those romantic eyes.

v

On this she sat forward with the apparent intention of scrutinizing him more closely. But, lowering for a moment her eyelids, she seemed to make an effort of memory. It was as though one who had acquired a knowledge of mechanics should recall, seeking to deduce its properties, some complicated toy he had possessed in childhood. "You've philandered disgracefully," she said at last. She nodded comprehendingly, as though she had found the key to him.

He spoke in an almost plaintive voice. "What would you have? I've always liked the society of women. And I've been so lonely. Lucia, you don't know . . . Away from home, like that . . . Sometimes, for months on end, there hasn't been a man I could talk to with sympathy. But a woman, that's different. At least they can give something—the passing illusion of affection." The smoke of his cigarette whirled out on a gusty sigh.

"Was that all? In so many years? Was there nothing more than that?" Her voice had an accent of pity.

By the space of an inch he too dramatically tossed his dark head. "I thought there was," he admitted. He ground out the coal of his cigarette with a sudden, twisting pressure. "I thought there was. Now —to-day—for the first time I realize there was not. Lucia, now that I've seen you, everything is clear. It *was* all just—illusion. I was seeking your image in them all. My dear, my dear." As abruptly he clasped her fingers, his voice dropped to a whisper. His eyes were turned from the brief mockery of the smile which startled the eagerness of her face. He crushed his parted lips against the back of her hand.

"I wish you hadn't said that!" she cried impulsively. "It's too perfect, your facility." She drew her hand slowly from his. She was trembling. "Forgive me, Luis," she went on. "My manners are disgraceful. And undoubtedly you meant what you said—yes, in a way, at this moment I am sure you mean it. As one so strangely may mean such things—for a moment." She gave a pitiful little laugh. "But I spoiled it, didn't I? It was unforgivable of me."

"Yes, quite," he said. He lowered his eyes, recovering with a sudden movement of the shoulders his accustomed air of melancholy poise.

She seemed to call up some reserve of gayety. "Yet after all," she brightly asked, "need we trouble? To impress each other, I mean. Think, Luis, after so many years? Or is that, perhaps, what made the quality, the particular fragrance of your speech?" She hesitated, lacing her hands tightly. "There are, you know, compensations in growing older. Things are simpler. One is no longer blown by every breath of charming emotion. People think I'm sentimental, you know. They make fun of me. But, Luis, my dear, I don't seem so dreadfully sentimental, do I?"

"Sentimental!" It was clear that he repudiated that. "You're made of stone," he dryly assured her. "Crystal, that's it. Hard and pure and cold. I've laid my broken heart at your feet," he told her casually. "And you don't care in the least." He lighted a fresh cigarette, one eyebrow raised, as though in fastidious avoidance of the ascending smoke.

"Oh, I do care," she declared with earnestness. It was evident that she reluctantly consented to acknowledge an emotion this moment held for her. "If not for your broken heart," she told him gently, "then for the fact that I once had a place there. For the fact that you would trouble to pretend I have a place there now. You won't believe me, Luis, but I'm deeply grateful to you." For a moment she paused, looking vaguely about the high, pale, unfamiliar room. "These things mean more to women than they willingly admit," she continued in a low voice. "I don't think they ever quite go to waste—not the silliest tribute, not the most patent flattery. They're—they're a divine reassurance, like the rain. All kinds of pretty flowers spring up where kind words have fallen. You'll see. You will come to see, won't you? I hope you'll have some time for us this summer. We'll be in the country in a week. We should so love having you," she concluded, rather formally.

"I'd very much like to come." His smile held a reservation. "Although now I'm a little afraid of you. You're so sure of yourself, you know. So wise and rational. You're like these other poised, cynical women."

"Paula?" Clearly she could not resist it.

"Well, I wasn't thinking of her when I spoke. But she does, I suppose, seem sure of herself."

"Paula's charming, isn't she?"

"Oh, very charming."

"She's told me you've grown to be such friends."

"Yes."

"This is a pleasant place for summer week-ends. I suppose you'll be here often. So undoubtedly we'll meet, now and then."

"I object to your forcing me into a false position." He gave her a baffled, offended look. "I see very well what you're getting at. I came here this week-end to see you. If that's rude to my hostess, I can't help it. You shouldn't make me say such things."

"But Paula told me that herself. Apparently you have been the soul of honor."

"Thank you. Besides, I've scarcely seen Paula since I arrived. She spent the morning talking with a Mr. Meyer."

"Yes, Herman Meyer."

"Who is he—an artist, I think?"

"Yes, he's done some fascinating work in the theater. Sets, you know, and costumes. Paula's been helping him with the costumes for a new production. Naturally they have to talk things over."

"He's here a great deal, I gathered."

"Herman? Well, yes. So many people are.

Revel and Paula, you see, are fond of company.
They always have a crowd about. Oh, I'm afraid
you have old-fashioned ideas, Luis. I just discern
a criticism in your tone."

"You're quite wrong. I don't know what you
mean. It's very unjust of you to say that."

vi

"You were always too sensitive," she said after a
pause. "It was a great weapon. You could always
get me to say I was sorry—even when it was most
evidently your fault. Because I couldn't bear to see
you silent and unhappy."

He lifted his head. "You'll laugh," he said, in his
low caressing voice, "but there are moments of that
summer I'll never forget. Moonlight on the lake—
oh, it's banal, I know, you've probably forgotten."
But he laid his fingers over hers.

"No," she said softly. She looked straight before her, with wide misty eyes, as though his words
had evoked something for her. "I haven't forgotten.
It was perfect, so youthful and romantic—intangi-
ble. Mystical and unfulfilled. I can still remember
quite clearly lines from the letters you wrote me.
How vulnerable a girl is! Oh, it *is* better, being
older! One suffers so much less. They swept me,
those letters, and certain shy, sentimental words of
yours shook me so that I could think of nothing else.
I suppose it's the same for every one. The first

trembling consciousness of emotion." Her fingers still rested passive in his clasp.

"Luis!" Paula's voice came sharply from the porch, and their fingers darted apart. "Luis French! Where are you?"

"Will you excuse me?" he murmured, and went to the door.

Lucia rose, too, with a small, indulgent smile. She walked vaguely to one of the farther windows, where she stood looking out for a moment on the ragged bushes which interposed between the croquet lawn and the house. She was still trembling a little. Ah, I was once so young, so tenderly, beautifully young! she cried; and she covered her face with her hands, filled with the pity and the regret with which a woman remembers the girl she has been.

CHAPTER VII

i

A GIRL with close-cut auburn curls ran toward the house. "I'll be five minutes," she softly sang. "Five little minutes. Five little scampering mice. Five gray little minutes."

With the arrival of Emmy and Randolph and Adrian, the group on the side-porch had scattered. Only Sackett East and a girl in a batik tunic still lounged on the orange cushions, apparently absorbed in an exchange of melancholy confidences. Randolph and Emmy and two wistful young men with sideburns had engaged in a croquet match which attracted a number of onlookers, and for their convenience wicker chairs had been drawn under the shade of a great maple. From these onlookers Jay detached himself, as Lucia deliberately skirted the green turf of the lawn.

"We're going swimming," he announced. He nodded toward the auburn-haired figure which ran up the steps of the porch. "Penelope and I aren't afraid of cold water." The prospect of activity seemed to hearten him, and he straightened his shoulders with an impatient movement, giving Lucia a small, intimate smile, as he strode away.

"So we meet again!" cried a boisterous voice; and Lucia saw that Adrian stood at her elbow. She nodded to him, accepting the chair he provided. "You cannot avoid me," he told her. "We are fated to meet, dear Lucia."

It was evident that she was not giving him her attention. She glanced toward the water. "I suppose it will be awfully cold," she vaguely murmured, as though she felt a necessity for saying something. Her eyes wandered after Jay, as he followed the straggling path to the bath-house at the water's edge. Dropping away beyond the tidy precincts of the wickets, the terraces were green and unkempt. Jay descended slowly, pausing at the tennis court to speak to Revel and Luis French. Then he passed under a tall willow, and was lost to sight behind the even line of a box hedge.

"Dreadfully cold, Mrs. Fanning, I assure you." Lucia started, and turned toward the speaker, whose voice betrayed an eagerness to please, to agree. "I simply put in my hand, it was like ice," he went on, gazing confidingly at Lucia with his sloe eyes. He had the mollified Jewish profile of a llama. There was a curly black mustache, as downy as a kitten's ear, above his small, semi-circular smile. His hands were very beautiful. He stood hesitating, caught in a moment of suspense, ready to accommodate himself to anything; looking with his soft, voluptuous face, like a king in Babylon of an effete period when there were no wars.

"Come, Herman, sit down, darling," said Paula; and she crushed herself against one side of her wide wicker chair, so that there was room in it for Herman, too. Around his shoulder, she tilted her head at Lucia, her apricot lips protruding. "You've been talking to Luis French," she accused her. "He told me when he came out. To think I *interrupted* you! Please forgive me, dear. But Revel was looking for him everywhere, to play tennis. I hope I didn't spoil too perfect a moment?"

"Quite perfect, Paula dear. But there will be others." She dismissed her sister-in-law serenely and competently. Meeting Adrian's gaze, she suddenly smiled. He laughed heartily, running his fingers through the vivid crest of his hair.

"Oh, Lucia!" he roared. "You're delightful. That mask of yours. It can't be displaced. You must teach me your secret." And, leaning over, he looked searchingly into her eyes.

"Lucia's sophisticated," said Herman, beaming agreeably at his own statement.

Eva had strayed languidly toward them. "Lucia sophisticated?" she asked. She sat on the arm of Lucia's chair, tightening her thin lips, which were painted a dry scarlet. "Oh, I think not. She always says and does the right thing, of course. But she's so full of sentiment. Positively, when I'm with her, I feel a hundred years old. There's a sweet childishness about Lucia," she went on, appealing to the others. "It's incredible. This week-end thing, now——"

Paula, peeping around Herman's shoulder, was eager to reply. "But that's just her *technique*. Don't you realize that? Fancy your being a novelist and not seeing *through* her! She's so uncannily clever. She gets every one's admiration." Paula raised her drooping eyelids on Lucia's air of gentle abstraction. "Men adore it. She has Jay completely tied, haven't you, darling?"

ii

She was on her feet with an air of mild surprise that she had risen. "What is it?" Adrian asked her, rising, too. "What do you want, Lucia?"

"I'm restless," she confessed. "You're all being so charming about me. I'm diverted. But I want to move about. Would any one take a walk?"

"Of course," said Adrian. He drew her hand through his arm and, accompanied by Eva, they moved across the graveled drive to the house. After a moment, Herman and Paula more slowly followed. "There's Penelope!" Adrian cried; and they stopped to observe the slender woman who skipped from the house, tossing her copper-colored curls. She was in the early thirties and her cheeks were wan. But she had large, shallow, misty eyes, and a fervent, curving mouth. She was wearing a short, close-fitting garment of white wool, bound at the waist with a belt of white. Her legs were bare, and on her feet were sandals which crossed her toes with narrow strips of silver. Between the strips appeared the shining vermilion of her painted toenails.

She had a pensive smile for them, pausing at the foot of the steps with her hands clasped over her small breast. She stood very straight, knees and feet pressed together. "I have silver shoon," she told them, speaking in a careful, childish voice. She peeped down at her feet, puckering her mouth into a red rosette.

"Penelope, you're *divine!*" caroled Paula. She put out her hand, as though to detain this bright presence. But Penelope evaded her. On sprightly feet she danced to the steps which led to the descending path. "Penelope's a dolphin, a silver, silver dolphin!" she sang, quite madly.

"But a week-end honeymoon, an anniversary picnic—well, there's something almost touching about it, isn't there?" Eva went on speaking, as though there had been no interruption.

"Quite. Oh, I quite agree—" Adrian began. But Lucia interposed.

"I won't hear any more! Not another word! Can't Jay and I spend a week-end together without suffering such a storm of abuse? Or rather, he doesn't suffer. I'm the only one. Why don't you attack him? He's going to the Farm just as much as I am." The last words were spoken almost absently, as she gazed beyond the terraces at the glitter of brilliant water. Over the emerald of the swamp grass the long pier extended, its props rising gauntly above the receded tide. A figure ran along the pier. "There goes Penelope," she murmured. "Oh, there's Jay coming back to meet her. Let's wait and see them dive."

In silence, the three strolled to the head of the brick steps, which led down to the tennis court, Paula and Herman, unnoticed, had disappeared. The swimmers gained the end of the pier, and Penelope clambered over the side.

"They'll dive from the float, of course," exclaimed Adrian. "We shan't be able to see them."

But Lucia shook her head. "I think Jay will dive from the spring-board. Although the tide is low," she added dubiously.

"It's always deep at the end of that pier," he assured her. "At whatever tide."

Jay had stepped on the spring-board which thrust its tongue from the top of the pier; and in a moment his body described a perfect curve to the water.

"How beautifully he dives!" Eva cried. "Oh, Jay is superb, isn't he? He can do anything."

"Yes, he does dive well." Lucia was almost excited. She glowed and smiled. Yet her eyes were a little anxious, she bent her head forward. "I think I see them in the water," she said uncertainly, her forehead wrinkling with the intensity of her scrutiny. Eva had turned away, and Adrian leaned close to her.

"Ah, sweet lavender," he whispered. "Can't you even let him leave you to go in swimming?"

She faced him, flushing, a little confused. "Well, why don't we take our walk? I'm quite ready. Shall we look at the rose garden?" she suggested to Eva. They moved at a leisurely pace around the side of the house, in the opposite direction to the croquet lawn.

"It's rather lovely and neglected," Eva said sadly, as they passed between the first tangled bushes. The women drew their light skirts about them, out of the reach of the briars. The early roses were already in bloom, and the leaves of the budding bushes gave out a sharp fragrance. Lucia bent over the slender stone sun-dial in the center of the garden and, parting the smothering brambles, disclosed the delicate bronze rose which ornamented the top. In such obscurity it had the aspect of a rare and hidden treasure. The garden was very still. No sound came from the house which, save for the white gables, was hidden from view by a high hedge and a grove of trees. The leaves of the bushes lightly rustled, and there was a faint, irregular humming of insects.

Adrian straddled a narrow stone seat, and produced a cigarette. Eva sank down beside him, laying her thin, dry hand on his arm. "Give me a light, too," she said. "Have one, Lucia?" But the younger woman shook her head. In the melancholy quiet, she strolled toward the farther end of the garden, which overlooked a tree-shaded lawn. Here the ground fell away gently from the slight elevation of the garden; and directly beneath was a rectangle of sheared grass, sometimes in use as a badminton court.

She stood idly gazing down on the pretty court. Then her attention sharpened as she observed beside it a bench on which were seated Paula and Herman Meyer. He was talking to her with smiling animation; his soft, soft little black mustache was close to her face. As she answered Herman, Paula laid one eager hand on his knee. Her pale blonde head was lightly tilted, before she dipped it for an instant to his shoulder. Then she raised her mouth to his.

Lucia had started to part the bushes, as though she intended calling out to them. But she abruptly turned, and walked back through the rose garden, more quickly than she had come. She scarcely paused at the stone bench, where Eva and Adrian still sat. "Come, let's go to the house," she said. "This place is too quiet. It's depressing. And it must be time for tea."

iii

On the side-porch, Emmy and Randolph idly watched a maid arranging the tea things. They had quickly tired of their croquet and the wistful young men. Emmy was smoking Randolph's pipe with evident relish; but, now and then, she paused and, wrinkling her nose, agitated her pink tongue, like a kitten lapping milk.

"Fancy," she greeted Lucia. "Only fancy! The horrid things actually like to smoke them!" Her fingers fell to winding the hair on either side of her face into demure taffy spirals. "Scene in a Vicarage Garden!" she cried, enjoying herself enormously. "I say, Ran! Look! Scene in a Vicarage Garden!" And putting the pipe to her lips, she exquisitely blew out a frail thread of smoke.

The maid brought hot water and a covered plate of muffins. "You do the tea, Lucia," said her brother. But she shook her head, as he drew a chair to the tea table.

"This is a holiday for me," she said; and impermanently she sat down on the edge of the long wicker sofa. "Eva will have to preside."

"Ah, yes!" Randolph accepted this with enthusiasm. "That's a good idea. Eva looks so charming, making tea. There, just see her! Like the Madame of a *very* high-class disreputable house, who's made a tidy fortune and can afford to do things properly. See her, spearing that lemon! No respectable woman could have such an elegant wrist." He handed a cup of tea to his sister. "You're feeling all right, aren't you?" he asked her in a lowered voice. She gave him a careless assent, turning to Adrian who had seated himself at her side.

Sackett East came from the house with a worried air, his fingers still caressing the pale, blurred flesh beneath his chin. "Have you seen Paula?" he demanded.

Randolph told him that they had not, and Adrian added that she was somewhere with Herman. The great man frowned nervously. "I have something I want to ask her," he muttered, and went off toward the croquet lawn.

Emmy giggled. "Poor old thing! Always fearfully ill about something, isn't he?" With an effect of caution she whispered, "What sort of person is Mrs. Sackett East? Why does one never see her?"

"Because she's at home," declared Adrian. "Where every woman ought to be. With her Little Ones." And he looked triumphantly at Lucia, as though he had scored a point.

"Does any one know her?" Emmy persisted. Her round eyes opened wide. "Is she pretty?"

"Yes, she's pretty." Randolph dubiously took it up. He hesitated, searching for an epigram. "In that honest, dependable way associated with strawberry festivals, monogamy and dark blue taffeta." On this he lighted a cigarette with an air of quiet satisfaction.

"I wondered," said Emmy. She had assumed an experienced manner, like a little girl who plays at being grown-up. "Because he's always having these rather poetic love-affairs. Like the one with Hallie Ennes."

"Oh, that's over," Eva said. "I understand," she added, raising her thin eyebrows, "that they're not actually love-affairs. Just a communion of soul with soul. Entirely frustrated."

"So that's the trouble!" said Emmy wisely.

"Yes, that's the trouble," Randolph assured her; and he gave his high, quick laugh, like a pleasant whinny.

iv

An influx of persons deflected the conversation. The two wistful young men had come from the croquet lawn, looking English and much in need of tea; and Paula brightly appeared, crying, "What shall we do to-night? Oh, Eva darling," she went on, "you're an angel, it's too divine of you to bother about the tea. I've been detained," she explained. Clasping her hands at the base of her throat, she appealed to them all. "Now we must *plan!* Let's have a marvelous party, something really imaginative. Jay, you big, beautiful thing, all red and damp and *healthy,* you aren't going to leave Paula to-night? You're going to stay, you know you are!"

Jay had entered the porch with his customary air of quiet confidence. It was expressed most clearly in the lift of the chin with which he looked about him, seeming not so much to join the group as to relate its members to himself. Apparently his swim had refreshed him, for his face looked younger; it was as though a relaxing hand had been passed over the tautened muscles of his brow and eyes. With an economy of movement, he dropped a piece of ice in a glass and mixed himself a Scotch and soda from the tray which stood on a low table.

Penelope drifted from the house, clad in draperies of pale orchid. Her lips were a varnished scarlet; her copper curls looked like wet mahogany. Above the purple chiffon scarf which she had wound about her bare throat, her cheeks were very pale. She darted to Jay's side. "For Penelope?" she begged, twinkling thin fingers toward the glass.

Jay relinquished it, set himself to the preparation of another highball. He had not answered his small sister-in-law, had merely bent upon her an intermittent and quizzical gaze. At last he said, "I've an appointment to-night with a beautiful woman. Sorry, Paula." Raising his glass, he bowed to Lucia with a barely perceptible movement of the lips—a wise, secret, intimate smile.

v

"Lucia, I protest. You're paying no attention to me. I can tell. Your eyes are roving all around. So are your thoughts. Are you trying to hear what the others are saying? It's very rude. Listen to me. This morning in the studio——"

"Oh, Sackett darling, come help us think what we should *do* to-night! Why, you poor old thing, I've been right *here*. Yes, I have, every minute of the time. Except for just the tiniest moment when I had to see the gardener——"

"—because if I offended you this morning, I'll apologize. But you have to listen to me, I can't apologize unless you listen. Why do you suppose I am sitting here with you on the sofa? I am trying to create a little emotional scene. It doesn't interest you at all. It's useless, it's disgusting. I've lost my charm. You sit there with that terrible vague smile of yours, that admirable, self-contained, Fifteenth Century smile——"

"—and I'm so dreadfully *sorry*, Sackett darling. Why didn't you tell me before? Yes, I do remember, last night she seemed a little queer, but I thought nothing *of* it. Well, why don't you telephone her right now——"

"—and it's all the more disquieting because you've been having a sentimental moment with that old beau of yours, that dark, taciturn, rather sissy type who's playing tennis with Revel. Is he going to come between us, Lucia? I was dreadfully torn when I arrived, and found that you were with him in the living room. Some one peeked and saw you together. There was quite a lot of talk about it. I almost came in and interrupted you. Would you have been angry with me, I wonder? Perhaps you like men to be masterful. Though Jay's manner with you—one couldn't really call it masterful. You're so beautifully—and a little ironically—polite to each other. I wish I understood you. There's

Penelope, lying in the hammock in a most abandoned attitude, and Jay's sitting beside her, and you don't seem to be noticing——"

"—but Sackett! Wait a minute. If she'd like to come, I'd simply love to have her here, you know. Ask her to come for the week-end. There's always room for one more. And, if she's upset and nervous, it might do her good to——"

"—because indifferent wives, I understand, and jealous wives, I understand. But if you aren't going to be either, it's most discouraging, because——"

"Look here, what's all the mystery? I took that fascinating woman home last night, and I think I have a right to know what's wrong with her. I have a feeling that Sackett's mixed up in it somehow. Come, Sackett, own up you have a guilty conscience——"

"Randolph darling, you don't keep *up!* That's been over for ages. They're just *friends* now."

"How affecting! Just friends? Well, well. How quaint! I wonder if she'd make friends with me. I didn't make much progress last night. Oh, but she has a strange and wonderful voice! There are bed-springs in it——"

"Oh, you horrid *thing!*"

Randolph raised his shoulders in an exaggerated deprecation. "I intend, I assure you, the highest compliment." He kissed his clustered finger-tips with reminiscent eyes. "Bedsprings arranged for the violin," he murmured ardently.

vi

"It's contended, you know, by some authorities that marriage ought to be monotonous. That it's the desirable as well as the inevitable thing. Perhaps they're right. Here, let me do that. Do you want charged water, Penelope?"

"Thanks terrifically. I got rather chilled swimming, didn't you? Just put that coat over me, would you? This *is* a stiff one. But, you see, I can't endure monotony. There's something in me—here——"

"Ah, well, you're still young. You'll settle down. You're not ready yet, that's all. Do you know, I felt that in you at once? It's in your voice. I notice a woman's voice directly. All her emotion is there, all her sex. But I'll tell you—do you want a piece of advice from an old man? Don't marry till you're ready to accept monotony. Otherwise you'll be rebellious—even if it's a good marriage, as marriages go. You may throw the relation out of gear. Oh, strange, subtle things happen between married people. But, you know, I think a lot of the fault lies in our sentimentalizing marriage too much. Especially women. They come to it, poor things, looking for some abstraction they call romance——"

"Penelope likes romance."

"Well, Penelope finds plenty of it, doesn't she? I tell you, my dear child, marriage isn't romance at all. It's the negation of it—it's permanence and security, a workable social and economic arrangement. It may produce great friendship, and the deepest affection. Oh, it's a wonderful state, don't imagine I'm disparaging that——"

"But I'm in love with Keats, you see. Haven't I ever told you that? It's quite too beautiful. Too beautiful. But it holds me back, I don't seem able to love any one else completely."

vii

Randolph smoothed with his palm the crisp black hair on the back of his narrow head. He sat at ease on the porch-rail, the long cylinder of a highball glass in one hand. "My friends," he said, "discretion is the only virtue. It has been called"—he paused for a sip from his glass—"the virtue of kings."

"Oh, be still, can't you?" said Sackett crossly. It was evident as he reluctantly advanced from the house, slamming the screen door behind him, that he chafed under a familiar friction.

"Yet the mind which could conceive that epigram," Randolph happily pursued, "which could endow a *Lady Minerva* with the subtlest, the most exquisite circumspection, seems totally unable to avoid betraying itself. Isn't it bizarre?" he demanded seriously of Eva.

"I was about to remark that the galled jade winced," she said, mincing her words nicely.

"Because, you see,"—Randolph held his audience for another leisurely sip—"even if he doesn't break down and tell All, he has always his guilty air. Just now he rushed into the house for a moment. Another man might do that without suspicion. Not Sackett. He comes out in such blushing confusion that a child would suspect him. This one does. He went to telephone a woman! Oh, Sackett, pull yourself together, old man. Is this civilized? What would *Lady Minerva* say?"

The unhappy playwright glowered from the depths of his chair. "You think you know so much," he told Randolph. "But you're wrong, you glib young whippet. Wrong again, like most multiloquous fools. You might find out more than you mean to, one of these days. I *did* go to telephone a woman—a long distance call and, when it's completed, I'm going in again to talk to her. That'll give you another chance to show your wit." He paused, breathing heavily. "He heard me speaking to you about it," he complained in an aside to Paula. "My heart is very bad to-day," he went on, and he laid a large hand on his waistcoat with a look of alarm. Then, drawing a large gold watch from his pocket, he proceeded with clumsy fingers to take his pulse.

viii

Adrian's hearty whisper was close to Lucia's ear. "Listen, sweet thing. Lean over. No, it's nothing wrong. Am I so unattractive that you cannot bear to come near me? I just want to be friends with you, kiss and make up. Well, at any rate, make up. And I want to give people the impression that there's something between us. God knows, there's nothing. Your thoughts are not for me. If you were watching Jay, I could understand it. That would be a very wifely thing. But you aren't watching Jay! Ah, you think I'm absurd, don't you? But look at Penelope. I beg of you, look at Penelope. She is more absurd than I am. She is having her third highball. Her lips are very passionate. Perhaps you'd like a highball, Lucia?"

She looked at him in that way she had, a long disconcerting stare, which seemed to see nothing. Penelope's small contralto voice sounded sleepily from the hammock.

"I'm very unhappy, Jay. Unhappy. Yes. I have my dream lover, my dream happiness—but sometimes, oh, you don't know, I feel things so——"

"I don't think I'd have anything more to drink, if I were you, my dear. You're half asleep, you know. Or perhaps you don't know."

"What's the matter with Penelope?" called Adrian.

Randolph explained. "She's in love with Keats. Hadn't you heard?"

"How nice for him!" Adrian leaned forward,

looking helpful. "Oh, Penelope! I've heard the Angel Gabriel well spoken of."

ix

"Sackett! Where's Sackett? Oh, did he go into the house again? Well, hasn't anybody thought of anything to do tonight? I don't think you're very much interested——"

"Paula! Look here. She's on the wire now. What shall I say to her? Shall I really ask her——"

"Why, certainly, tell her I'd love having her. But insist on her *coming*, Sackett. Don't let her stay all alone in town. Listen, everybody, Hallie Ennes is coming out. Isn't that divine? Sackett's making her come because she's all alone in town, with nothing to do. I think she's the most fascinating person!"

x

"They're all making fun of me, Jay. All except you. You're right, you know, that Scotch has made me terrifically sad. And I felt so exhilarated when I was swimming. Now I'm in a sort of twilight world. Nothing is real. Did you ever feel like that?"

"I don't think I ever did, exactly, Penelope. It sounds like a rather feminine feeling. But I can imagine it's most uncomfortable."

"No, it isn't quite that. Not quite uncomfortable.

In a way, it's really lovely, awfully vague and beautiful. Like sitting by the sea or having tears in your eyes or listening to unseen music. Or that sad, sad, *precious* moment, just before you go to sleep. I love the quality in life of vagueness, ambiguity. People say it's in my verse. Oh, I'm afraid sometimes I wasn't meant for real life at all. I've been bewitched. I'm fey. I can't belong to anybody, not anybody. And I don't want to. Oh, I couldn't bear to think of being married, tied to some man, having him always there, having him *sure* of me——"

"My dear little girl! No man should ever be so unwise as to feel sure of a beautiful woman."

CHAPTER VIII

i

"To think," Luis murmured, "that I came here to-day to see you!"

As though vaguely touched by his plaintive tone, Lucia turned to him with a little gesture of compunction. She had just run into the house for her gloves; and, catching sight of her from the corner of the porch, he had come to supplement their sufficiently formal good-bye.

"It's unsatisfactory, isn't it?" she said. "So many people. Such chatter! It was scarcely the place to renew an old friendship. But we'll make up for it later on. I have your promise that you'll come to us, you know."

The gravel of the path made a muffled crunching under their tread, as they moved toward the driveway where Jay and Revel stood talking. Brightly on the path Paula sped before them, and the brothers turned to receive her with an effect of patience. Her high voice floated back, "But what in the world do you *see* in that lonesome place? It's going to be such fun here tonight! If you're bored, Jay, run down after dinner. Promise Paula——"

"It's good-bye, then," said Luis abruptly. They

were drawing close to the others, and he stepped ahead, so that she was obliged to pause. "What is it?" he asked, scrutinizing her face. "Why are you so preoccupied? Is it just that you're bored with me?"

"No, no," she said; and she tried for a moment to give him her wandering attention. "You must forgive me, Luis. I'm sure I seem rude. It's absurd," she added, with an apologetic laugh, "but I feel quite tired. I'm eager to get away. I'll be very different next time, you'll see." She pressed his hand, half-turning from him, so that even his scarcely prolonged pressure of her fingers had the effect of detaining her. But, as though regretting her impulsive haste, she at once looked back at him, nodding and smiling.

"Good-bye, beautiful lady," he said. He tossed his dark head, and went quickly toward the house.

She had taken her place in the car, and Jay tucked a light rug about her knees. Paula fluttered on the running board, bending over her. "Lucia, where did you get those marvelous *bracelets?* Well, aren't you the luckiest person! Revel, look what Jay gave Lucia. Aren't they *divine?*"

ii

The car swung heavily up the drive, and plunged along a stretch of clear, tree-bordered road. The cool, sweet afternoon air fanned their faces, and

Lucia drew a deep breath. "All right, beautiful lady?" Jay inquired; and meeting his eyes, seeing his wise, secret smile, she put back her head with a free gush of laughter.

"Oh, dear," she said regretfully, at last. "A man changes in ten years. I wonder if I've changed as much. Or perhaps the change is actually in me," she admitted. "In my perceptions, sharpened to see the pattern of a man like Luis. Yet it's different in a boy. Youth, I suppose, is the time for romantic gestures. One believes in them then." She sighed a little sadly. "One would like to believe in them now. All the lovely words, the sentiments, the beautiful promises."

"Oh! So he made you beautiful promises?"

"Try not to be absurd, dearest." She lightly patted his gloved hand which rested, casual and competent, on the steering wheel. "I'm so glad to get away!" she cried. "I thought the afternoon would never end."

"I don't see how we could have left much earlier, do you?"

She met this promptly. "Oh, no. We had to stay. But when you said you thought we should go—I nearly cried for joy. Sometimes so much confusion is tiring. You have to be *outside* yourself to enjoy a chattering crowd. And I seem very much *inside* myself today. I understood how nervous people can't endure being in crowds. The voices were all in my head. Like a crazy phonograph record. I couldn't talk. I just sat there hypnotized by the noise."

He looked at her. "You're rather pale. I noticed you were quiet. I thought perhaps you had a headache."

"It isn't exactly a headache. Oh, it's all my own fault. I should rest more. I let myself get nervous and strained and over-emotional. I've been quite jumpy all day. Did you have a nice time?"

"Yes, pleasant enough. Penelope's amusing. She's a little mad."

"That's just it, that's just what I mean, Jay. They all seemed a little mad. Oh, I'm sure it was my mood. They couldn't be any different than usual. But I wasn't amused to-day. Everything they said seemed so false, artificial, fantastic. Do you know what I mean?"

"Yes, I know what you mean. But I didn't have your reaction to it. You're feeling nervous and out of sorts. That makes the difference."

"Yes, I know. But—it's something more than that, too, I think. Haven't you ever felt quite sickened by flippancy and pretense and affectation? So that you could scarcely bear it? So that you wanted to cry from your heart—to tear it out, almost, and expose it, quite naked. Then there would be one real thing among you. One thing too real, I mean, to lie about or laugh at." She sat forward tensely, looking at her clasped hands. Then she slid down in her seat. "I do sound rather hysterical," she said apologetically.

iii

"I'm awfully ashamed." She spoke meekly, out of a silence of several minutes. "I've been acting like a spoiled child all day. This morning, you know, I ran out of the house to get away from Aunt Geraldine. It was dreadful of me. But I was so restless. It didn't seem possible to clear my mind, and make way for Aunt Geraldine's conversation. I suppose it's old-fashioned selfishness. It used to be so simple, didn't it? You could cover a thousand nervous complaints with one explanation. Now no one mentions selfishness at all. It isn't the fashion. It's unscientific."

"Very *declassé*. I'm surprised to hear the word on your lips."

She was still seriously considering it. "We've learned to excuse everything, that's what it comes to. Being scientific is so easy and pleasant. All the old-fashioned virtues are outlawed. There's fidelity, for instance—that's degenerated into practically a perversion."

Jay seemed to await a further development. "Well, what then?" he at last said.

"Only that—why, dearest, as I've thought over this morning (with a kind of compunction, I sup-

pose, because I ran away) Aunt Geraldine seemed
to me such a pathetic figure. She has no life, no
real personal life, of her own. Her happiness, almost her only contact with experience, comes through
her relation to you and Revel. But he counts far
less, because you're so clearly the one she worships.
Actually, Jay, we're responsible for Aunt Geraldine's
happiness——"

"Is that why you left her this morning?"

"No, dear. Don't laugh. I don't mean in little
things, but quite fundamentally. It's true of
Mamma, too, in just the same way. There are two
of them. Their lives are so empty, Jay. They're so
dependent on us."

"Well?" Clearly the topic did not engage him.
"We'll have to put up with it, I suppose? We can't
stop them, can we?"

"You rather resent it, don't you? Though you're
the kindest person in the world. I think I know
why you resent it."

He waited. "Why do I?"

"Because it's a kind of interference. A curtail-
ment of your liberty. You'd like to be quite ruthless—behave as you pleased, say it was no one's
affair what you did. You hate, actually, that soft,
clutching tyranny of affection. Like an octopus
winding its tentacles around you. But you can't
escape, you poor darling. You aren't ruthless
enough."

iv

"Lucy. This is, of course, something very much between ourselves. I'm desperately concerned about Revel."

"Ah, I was sure of that. That was in my mind just now. Is it money?"

"Yes."

"Serious?"

"Terribly."

"Anything to do with the Hagerman failure?"

"Yes. How did you guess? Revel was involved. Well, practically everything he has. That's all. He didn't tell me until to-day. I don't know that anything could have been done, anyway. Funny, I never suspected, until I saw his face this afternoon. Then I knew there must be something wrong —something considerably more than the few thousands he lost last month. Oh, my dear, it's tragic. What luck he's had! And a wife like Paula!"

"Does she know?"

"Not yet. God help Revel when she does."

"Ah, poor Revel. He's such a dear. Why does that kind of fine sensitive person have all the bad luck?"

"While a hard-boiled bastard like me prospers? My dear, I don't know. I've often wondered."

"But, darling, if it weren't for the hard-boiled people, what would happen to the others? After all, you're able to help Revel. Let's be glad of that.

You know, dearest—well, of course, you wouldn't hesitate to tell me anything that was necessary? I mean, if it's desirable for a time, any change, any retrenchment——"

"My dear, there's no question of that. No question at all. I have plenty of money. Why, the whole thing would be simple, if I could just hand him a check. But I hesitated to do that today. I felt it would be tactless—not the right thing. It'll come to that in the end, of course."

"Is it inevitable Paula should know? Because, Jay, I don't suppose we can imagine how she'll make him suffer. Oh, if we can, dear, let's keep Paula from knowing—ever. It'll be far worse than you think. Oh, I understand her so well. She's already so jealous of us because we have more than they have. If they're poor, if they have to take money from us, she'll hate us. She'll try to ruin your relation with Revel—not openly, of course, but in subtle, insidious ways. My dear, I *know* this. When a man like Revel marries a woman like Paula, he's unfortunate. When he loves her, he's ruined."

"I'm afraid, Lucy, you're right." Jay drew his breath audibly between his teeth. "Oh, God! We'll have to work it out somehow. Let's put it out of our minds for the moment. Look here, my dear, I feel as though I'd been rather a kill-joy all day. I was nervous myself this morning, just a bad mood. Now I feel better, I've snapped out of it. So let's have as nice a time as we can, what do you say?"

v

She gave him several furtive little glances, disguised by comments on the scenery. It was apparent that she was moved by a desire to speak, and once or twice her lips opened, only to close upon a sigh, evidently engendered by a repressing second thought. At last she said, "Do you love me, Jay?" She spoke quickly, casually, coaxingly, with an effect of humorous intention.

He pretended indignation. "I shouldn't think you would ask me such a thing. Certainly not. You are repellent to me. Often when I see people making a fuss over you, I wonder to myself: How can they possibly——"

"Don't tease. Tell me, you do love me, don't you?"

"Of course." He had finished with it, on that.

"But really, I mean. You know what I mean." She bit her lip, shaking her head impatiently, as though annoyed at herself. But she went on. "Deep in your heart, you do love me, as I love you, so that my life seems a part of yours?"

There was the faintest quiver in her voice, and he answered, "Your life *is* a part of mine, dear."

Again she paused, but she could not leave it. "I've been a good wife to you? There isn't anything you would change?"

"Nothing in the world." He was emphatic. "Have I ever tried to change anything about you?"

"No, never. No, I'm sure that you never have. Have I about you?"

He admitted an occasion for humor. "Certainly not. You're far too sensible."

"Do you remember—" She faltered over it. "Jay, do you remember——?"

"Do I remember what?"

"Do you remember that once you said to me— that I had never failed you?"

"Yes, Lucy. Yes, my dear. Of course, I re- member."

"You still—feel that same way?"

As though recognizing an obligation to the stifled entreaty in her voice, he turned to her. "Oh, my dear, I take those things for granted. Of course, I do." He seemed pained by his own slight impa- tience. "You're a wise person," he told her, "you should know those things without asking."

"Ah, I don't feel very wise today." She con- fessed her failure on a long sigh. She appeared to debate it with herself. "I'm not usually like this. I wonder what's the matter with me? It's idiotic, I suppose, but I'm hungry for words," she explained. "I can't defend it. But I want words terribly. I suppose we always do—women—but sometimes we conceal it better than others. Reassurance, I sup- pose. It's always reassurance we're all looking for, isn't it?"

He protested. "You've always said I spoil you with pretty speeches."

"Yes. Yes, you do, dear. But I didn't mean the pretty speeches so much. I adore them, of course. But they're the gallantries you pay to every woman, aren't they? I mean, there's actually nothing of your heart in them. Well, how absurd I am! Sorry, darling. Forget it." She patted his arm.

"Well, my dear, you know how much I admire you." He was evidently unwilling to leave her dissatisfied, but his tone was a little cursory, a little business-like. "You're wise. And beautiful. And intelligent. I don't know what more a woman can be. God knows I was wild enough when you married me. I must have given you many unhappy hours. Our marriage might so easily have smashed those first two years. You saved it. . . . And let's see. You never offend me. You're entirely sensitive. Reticent. Courteous. All the things that are pleasant to live with. Adaptable. You never seem to disapprove. . . . There's a whole catalogue of charms and virtues. What more can I say?"

"Nothing more." She laid her hand over his. "Thank you, dearest. I sound wonderful. Am I really as nice as that?"

vi

She was evidently prepared to take a lightly scoffing tone. "Ten years! Why should the fact of ten years be so important? It's a purely arbitrary division—a decade. Don't you see what I mean?"

"Quite. I've quite grasped it."

But she had more to say. "Still, you couldn't guess how I've sentimentalized this anniversary."

On this he was indulgent. "You're not very flattering. Have I lived with you so long without perceiving that you're just a quivering mass of sentiment? Nicely disguised, of course, with little dignities and reserves, airs of indifference, pretty manners."

"Oh. Loathsome expression, a quivering mass! You think that, because you have so little sentiment. Scarcely the tiniest scrap. Most men have a trace of the feminine in their natures. It's very engaging, too. Do you realize how entirely masculine, how hard-shelled and practical you are?"

"I ought to. You've told me often enough." He was inclined to bear the imputation cheerfully.

"But, after all, you're very tolerant of my sentimental attitude about us. You're quite willing to humor me in it. I don't think I've ever heard you complain."

"*I* should complain that a beautiful woman——?"

"Beautiful *lady*, dear."

"Ah, yes. Stupid of me. Beautiful *lady*. By all means."

vii

"I started to say something. What was it? Oh, yes, about sentimentalizing this anniversary. A minute ago, you said we might have smashed during the first two years. I suppose that's true. But it comes as a little shock when you say it. I wanted to contradict you. It sounded so absurd. You know, that's the part of our marriage that I always forget. Really, Jay, I do, I never think of it. That means, I suppose, that I don't want to remember. But that's rather silly of me. How does it matter? I'm sure that in every marriage there's such a time. The inevitable process of adjustment."

"Yes."

"But your saying I saved it—that's not true. It was so much of it my fault. I was so childish. Inexperienced. And I was twenty-two! I was an idiot. A romantic little fool. I didn't know what it was all about. And I was so stuffed with pruderies and prejudices and neat conventional ideas——"

"Yes, of course. That's why it's remarkable you managed the thing so well. What about me? I wasn't so young, you know. I thought I was a devil of a fellow."

"But, oh, my dear, it all came out all right. That was such a little part of our marriage. What did it amount to, actually? You took too much to drink a few times. I used to mind—oh, that was just for a few months—when you paid attention to other women. It wasn't that I was really jealous, you know. It was my silly, mid-Victorian feeling about marriage—and I kept thinking what Mamma would say if she knew!"

"I think she used to suspect sometimes that things weren't going well. But you never told her."

"Told her? Are you mad, darling? . . . But that was all so quickly past. I remember, I worked it out one night when you'd stayed out very late. It was before Nickie came. I'd never been able to make scenes, don't you know. I detest all that so. It was all bottled up inside me. You'd come home— a little happy, shall we say? In the most dignified and elegant and reticent way! You flung yourself into bed, and slept. I couldn't sleep. A lot you cared! You lay there so oblivious and peaceful. Oh, I haven't thought of that night in years! I got up—it was when we were in the apartment on Sixtieth Street—and stood for a long time looking down at you. There's nothing quite so annoying as a person who's distressed you and who lies serenely sleeping, like a baby after its bottle. (There's humor there, darling, but I won't develop it.) And I thought to myself: Well, I've married it. I thought, I love it more than anything in the world. And then I thought, if I kept on disapproving and suffering and sulking, I'd be like all the dreadful wives that ever lived. I thought that I was going to have a baby. And I thought about my own childhood, and Mamma crying and nagging until I wanted to die. . . . I saw everything very clearly and reasonably. And, even then, I had sense enough to know that you can't change people. You can only adapt yourself to them and be tolerant of them and get used to them. Well, that's about all. I was better after that. I'm always better once I've thought things out. I used to pray God to keep me from thinking I was always right. That developed a pretty humility in me."

She broke off with a laugh. After a moment, she went on, a little ruefully. "This isn't at all what I started to say! It's quite the reverse. I wanted to talk about the *real* part of our life together. All the things that have happened. All you've done for me. Dear! You've been so generous, so reasonable. All day I've been thinking about you. I've had waves of emotion about you. I've been trying to escape from them, to distract myself. But today I'm like something that's been skinned. All my nerve-ends are laid bare. The least touch is painful. . . . Everything in my life, Jay, when I think—Dear Archie, that will be six years next month, the fourteenth. . . . When I think how good you were then, how kind you were to Mamma. And Nickie was so ill then, too. I could never have borne it without you. Dear, it's silly of me to cry. I can't think why I'm behaving like this, because I'm really so happy, so terribly happy."

viii

They had left the level, gleaming highway for a dirt road, and over its uneven surface Jay drove more slowly. The scene through which they passed had a quiet, rustic beauty. Sometimes the narrow road led between close aisles of trees; again it opened on fields, bordered with tumbling stone walls, along which stretched the attenuate shadows of late afternoon. An occasional white farmhouse stood primly near the road. Against the paling sky the rounded crests of hills were starred with blossoming fruit trees.

A group of children played before a farmhouse door, and, looking at them, Lucia put her fingers hesitantly to her mouth. "I do hope Nickie has been all right," she murmured, uncertainly.

Jay was firm. "Of course, he's all right. Don't begin fussing about *that*. I'm glad you're going to get away next week. You're very nervous."

She accepted this as a reproach. "I'm not going to fuss," she assured him. She fumbled in her purse for her handkerchief, and unostentatiously dried her eyes. She drew a long breath, as she tucked the handkerchief into its place; folding her hands lightly over the purse, as though resolved to control their nervous movements. She raised her head and looked about her at the tranquillity of the homely scene, constantly repeating its suggestion of peace and repose. The quiet of early evening was like the pause in a slow respiration.

"Paula loves excitement," she at last irrelevantly said. "How extravagant she is! They always have a houseful of people. There's to be a big party to-night. Apparently your friend, Mrs. Ennes, is coming up. Did you hear that?"

He was casual. "Why, I did hear Sackett speak about telephoning her. Was it arranged?"

"Evidently. He said something about her being alone in town. He was most solicitous. Jay——"

"Yes?"

She hesitated over it. "I'm sorry about this morning. I must have sounded so petty and ungenerous. Let her keep my case, of course——"

He protested. "What are you talking about, my dear?"

"The case, the cigarette case. I'd like Mrs. Ennes to have it. I'm ashamed to think how mean I must have sounded—over such a trifle."

"My dear, you're absurd. It wasn't mean in the least. Don't make so much out of nothing. She simply forgot to return it, that's all. Of course, I'll get it back for you. It's your property." He had slightly raised his voice, in expostulation.

She was persistent. "But, Jay, I'd really like— I should feel better about it. Permit me this generous gesture." She implored it prettily. "It's so good for my soul."

"Not even for that exalted purpose. You'll have to take out your heroism in some other way."

She accepted the finality of his decision with a reluctantly admiring smile. "Oh, you're so uncannily wise! And so hard-hearted! You're not willing to let me feel the mild moral advantage which such generosity would give me."

He laughed at the grievance in her voice. "You're not such a fool yourself, my dear."

At such a moment, they seemed to understand each other very well. "As if I couldn't see through you!" she cried, almost gayly.

ix

A gradual turning brought into view a small, blind house, set above the road on a rock-strewn elevation. The dooryard was occupied by lilac bushes and the worn, white pergola of a well. This was the farmer's cottage on the Fanning property, a former barn, long since converted to living purposes. Farther on, the land sloped to the level of the road, and a short driveway led to the main house. Jay stopped the car, as a man, leaning heavily on a stick, lurched across the dooryard of the cottage. His blue shirt was opened on a gaunt, stringy neck. In his free hand he held the remains of a withered winter apple, most of which was stored in one cheek, where he preyed upon it at his leisure. He greeted the arrival of the car with a face as woebegone as this distortion would permit.

"What's the matter with Ed Pardee?" Jay exclaimed. "What's the trouble, Ed?" He jumped from the car, and approached the other, who gloomily shook his head.

"Cut my foot chopping." He thrust out the bandaged member. "Marie's got everything ready up to the house. Late, ain't you?"

"Yes, we are, rather. Sorry to hear you've been laid up. Have you had a doctor, Ed? Taking care of yourself all right?"

Ed was disposed to a mournful resignation. "Yes, I'm all right." As the apple was demolished, his long seamy face took on its accustomed symmetry. He hitched himself forward, greeted Lucia. "I just seem to get the hard end of everything," he complained. "I'll hobble over to the house later, to see if there's anything——"

Jay climbed into the car, shaking his head. "No, no, don't think of it. I'll run in and have a talk with you tomorrow. Don't think of coming up."

The car started forward, and slowly turned into the drive which led to the main house. "Isn't that perfect?" Lucia murmured. "Have you ever seen Ed when he hadn't something wrong with him? How do you suppose Marie stands it?" she wondered, as they stopped beside an old house, not greatly different, save for its more pretentious size, from the cottage they had just passed. Like all the houses along this road, it was high-shouldered and sedate, wearing an air of mean, self-contained dignity. Small effort had been expending on remodeling it; and for Lucia the Farm had always held possibilities of lovely transformation. In the rear was the commodious, low-ceiled kitchen, which looked on a pleasant close of apple trees; and walking under them, Lucia had often planned the flagged walk she would lay between springing rows of old-fashioned flowers. Heavy clumps of lilacs filled the air with fragrance. The hillsides behind the house were pale with the blossoming orchard. To the left a little lake glimmered between the trees.

Lucia looked about her. "You see," she said thoughtfully, "you could have a bricked terrace here, trellised with grapes and honeysuckle. The lovely smell, in summer and fall! You could eat out here, looking at the orchard and the lake. And the kitchen's so well arranged," she went on, "with the stove and sink hidden in that angle by the stairs. It's such an unbeautiful period, you shouldn't bother about its being American. It ought to be a peasant kitchen, with huge dressers, great shiny copper pans, pottery dishes, red printed cotton." As she laid her hand on Jay's arm, she was interrupted by a cheerful, comely woman of about thirty who appeared at the kitchen door. This was Ed Pardee's wife, Marie. She shook hands with the self-conscious cordiality of the country-bred.

"Too bad Ed's laid up," she told them, pleasantly. "But I don't know as you'll miss anything. I can do about anything Ed can do." She smoothed the front of her neat calico dress, the waist of which was tightly filled by her wide bosom. Her skin was fresh and ruddy. Her hair sprang vigorously from the neck and temples, still showing the clean sweep of the brush. "I got you a nice steak, see here, Mrs. Fanning. The potatoes are all boiled, you can hash-brown them if you want. I cooked you up some vegetables, too. And I made an apple-pie. You get up so seldom, I thought—" She beamed warmly upon them, to complete the sentence. "Now, if you like, don't hesitate to tell me, I can stay right on, and serve you your supper. What do you want with messing around a stove in that good dress?"

Lucia looked at the table, which stood in the center of the spotless kitchen, laid with a coarse white cloth, china of various patterns, a butter dish and spoon holder of heavy glass, and a cruet-stand. "No, thank you, Marie," she said. "I'll put on an apron. I like doing it. This is a picnic for us, you know. You've fixed everything beautifully. Is the stove working all right?"

Marie gestured capably toward it. "Stove's fine. There's only one thing. Did you see Ed? Did he say anything about the tank?" She received their denial with a shake of the head, her lip curling as she spoke of her husband with a kind of good-humored scorn. "Well, I thought he wanted to tell you himself, but I guess I might as well. Be careful of the water," she admonished them, impressively. "The tank's only half full. The pump ain't working." On this, she moved her head, with a look of intelligence for Jay, in the direction of the lake. "Seems Ed started pumping the other day, and he found one of the parts was broken. He had to send for it, he's been expecting it every day, but it hasn't got here yet."

"One of the parts broken?" Jay received it philosophically. "That's a nuisance. Still, if the tank is half full——"

"Maybe not half. I haven't been to look myself. I've had so much to do, with Ed crippled up. But I guess you'll make out all right," she told them cheerfully. She bent for a moment over the stove. "I'll be going along, then, if that's all. Your little boy keep well? Yes, thank you, mine are all well, thank the Lord. Yes, it is too bad about Ed. Seems he's always got to get hurt at the most upsetting times. But we got to take what we're sent." She reached the door on this, with a long sigh that lifted her heavy breast. "Let me know if there's anything you find you want," she urged them.

x

"Now, what a life!" Lucia protestingly cried, as the woman went along the path which led to the cottage. "That woman, Jay! How, *how* can she live with Ed Pardee? What did she ever see in him? Why, he isn't even clean. I can't believe she's his wife. But they have three children—she must have liked him once. Well, must have been able to stand him."

"You heard her say we've got to take what we're

sent." Jay's shrug expressed his willingness to leave it at that.

"Yes, but wouldn't you think she might have been sent something better than Ed Pardee? She's years younger. And quite a handsome woman. So vigorous and sensible. I wish I understood——"

He deprecated her evident distress. "My dear, get over the idea that you can ever understand why one person is magic to another."

"Ed Pardee *magic?* Jay, I must ask you——"

"Well, when she married him, he was different. I distinctly remember him as different." He took a pipe from his pocket, and slowly filled and lighted it, self-contained, undisturbed.

Lucia, nervously pressing her teeth into her lips, watched the deliberate motions of his hands. "She seems so contented," she murmured at last, and with a hopeless little gesture she dropped her gloves and purse on the table. "She has no illusions about Ed. You can see it when she speaks of him. But she's accepted her life somehow, hasn't she?" Her head bent, she looked down at the table-cloth with wide eyes, speaking in a low voice, which expected no reply. "She isn't struggling. Isn't torn. There's a tranquillity about her. I wonder if it's living in the country? I wonder if it's religion? It might be religion"—she pursued it softly—"that lovely, unquestioning acceptance."

Jay had his own thoughts, expressed with a tolerant disgust. "What an idiot, letting the pump get out of order. The tank's small at best. Still, Marie assures us we'll make out all right." He sauntered comfortably to the door, pipe in hand.

"Oh, yes," Lucia said vaguely. But she had a skeptical smile for his last words. "I wouldn't be too sure that the Pardee standards of making out accord with ours. You'd better go up the hill and have a look for yourself."

"I will, later on." He picked up their handbags, which he had dropped beside the door. "I'll just take these up before I do anything else."

She could hear his feet racing up the stairs, as she more slowly followed, pausing for a glance at the stiff, old-fashioned parlor. Marie Pardee had opened the shutters and thoroughly cleaned the room, but it still held a musty smell, the breath of disuse from the heavy old carpet, yellowed wall-paper, decaying pot-pourri. In the large back bed-room on the floor above, Jay had tumbled out his toilet articles, his pajamas and slippers and, contentedly surveying the disorder, he applied a fresh match to his pipe. His ruddy hair was not quite neat, and he stroked it with his brushes, squinting at the imperfect glass of the mirror. There was about him a satisfaction, almost a relief, that had not been present during the day. In contrast to his earlier preoccupation, his manner seemed youthful, almost boyish.

"You up here, too?" He affected to find this disturbing. "When do we eat?" he demanded, with a pretense of blustering, encouraged by Lucia's smile.

"In a minute," she said. She stood quite still in the middle of the bedroom, looking at him. "I'll be down in a minute."

"I don't like cooks," he grumbled, "who stand staring in bedrooms, when it's time for dinner." He produced his secret smile, which gave him the wise air of an old sea lion. "I'll just put the car away," he told her, and ran quickly down the stairs.

"I'll be down in a minute," she said again. Still she stood in the middle of the room, hearing his footsteps die away. She threw back her head, and pressed her fingers over her throat, as though stricken by the fear of an infinite pain.

xi

At once, on that other night, she had liked the farmhouse bedroom, with its low ceiling, square windows and uneven, painted floor. It was, she recognized, unchanged. There was the big mahogany bed which Marie had freshly made, a patchwork quilt doubled at the foot. There were the rag rugs, the chest of drawers surmounted by a faulty mirror, the framed motto, embroidered in crewel-work, on the wall above the bed. Outside one window, the branch of an apple tree brushed the pane with frail blossoms. Their two bags stood companionably on the floor. All, all was as it had been.

In the mirror, she dimly saw the reflection of her face. So imperfect was the image that she was startled, as though she had seen a stranger who closely resembled herself; as though this might be the other Lucia, the young one, who had come to this room as a bride. With her wide, dark eyes, she seemed caught, imprisoned behind the mirror in the neat, prim room where such violence had been done her. For she had not survived. She was surely not a part of the mature, experienced woman who had gradually taken her place; a woman to whom the estate of wifehood was the sum of existence.

Now to Lucia, standing passive in the farmhouse bedroom, the almost buried remembrance of that other night returned; and, closing her eyes, she allowed herself to be swept by the waves of memory. Her heart had pounded deliberately, like a rhythm of admonitory finger taps as, with an effect of reluctance, she had undressed in the faintly lighted room. From the bathroom had come the sound of running water and the brisk noise of Jay's toothbrush.

As she combed her dark hair, she had gravely examined her fine-spun nightgown, made by a Belgian nun. She had thought with pity of the bride of Christ, stitching for other women in a bare room beside a simple court. Patting the lace with shaky fingers, she had felt superior; a woman desired, beloved, possessed.

But as the sound of running water ceased, her timid self-importance had been pierced by a virginal dread of the unknown. Almost, for a moment, she had envied that calm nun; almost would have shared her dear security, stuffy and incensed with gentle prayers. Jay had come out of the bathroom and, seeing him in a dressing gown, she had fully sensed her panic before the inevitable. She had drawn her négligé about her shoulders; then fearing she might offend him, had dropped her hand.

He was, she had dimly realized, self-conscious. He had made conversation. "Such a lovely nightgown, darling. What do you call that, what lace?"

"Binche. Isn't it pretty? This is one of the things Mamma had made for me in Brussels." Her voice was not quite steady, but she had carried it off. Even then, a raw girl, she had known how to disguise her feelings; her pride had always been able to whip her into a show of composure.

xii

Lucia passed her fingers over her eyes, shaking her head. She opened her dressing case, and took out a jar of rouge, and rubbed a faint color on her cheeks. Suddenly she stepped into the hall, and peeped into the other bedrooms. They were neatly disposed, but the beds were unmade, the mattresses turned over the footboards. Marie Pardee had no modern ideas as to how a husband and wife should sleep.

As she fingered the things in her dressing case, the quiet of the country evening was like a presence in the room. Birds sang sharply, and at the windows the muslin curtains stirred. She gazed out at the lake, lying pale as a moonstone amid the dense encircling foliage. She could see the little dock, the row-boats beside it, the overturned canoe, and the small shack which housed the pump.

Her fingers grasped the smooth, substantial footboard of the bed, while a slow minute passed. "Perhaps it's the country," she murmured; "this perfect quiet. In the city we give out too much, we're wasted in little squandering contacts. . . ." Her eyes fell on the framed motto above the bed. Coarsely worked in tomato red and grass green wools, with an immense, elaborate initial, ran the words, "He Will Not Leave Thee, Nor Forsake Thee." "Perhaps it's religion," she cried. She bent over the footboard, covering her face with her hands. Tears dropped between her fingers. "God, God," she whispered, "help me to take what I'm sent."

xiii

She hurried down to the kitchen. Jay stood in the doorway, his face turned toward the sunset.

"Did I seem long?" she asked him. "I unpacked a little. I'm sorry I kept you waiting. But there's only steak and potatoes to get ready. I won't be five minutes. You'll see, not five minutes, my only darling!"

CHAPTER IX

i

JAY appeared to speak out of a moment's consideration. "Do you know what I'm thinking of doing?"

"What are you thinking of doing?"

"I want to buy this place from Revel."

"Jay!" She put down her fork, looking at him intently. "Not really?"

"You'd like that, wouldn't you?"

"Like it!" Her smile, her lighted eyes answered him. "It's as though you'd read my thoughts. I've always wanted this place to be ours. Now—it's rather a solution, isn't it?"

He acknowledged this interpretation. "Exactly. Don't you see? It's a fairly valuable property. And Paula cares nothing about it, she'll be delighted to have it sold. I'm convinced Revel's held on to it out of sentiment. In this way, it remains in the family. He can still use it. Oh, it's an excellent idea. I don't know why I didn't think of it at once."

"You aren't afraid he'll see through it as a plan to help him?"

His eyebrows lifted. "My dear, I'm not afraid of any one's raising many obstacles in the way of some-

203

thing he desperately needs. Besides, I'll put it up to him with tact. Naturally." For a brief space he scrutinized it. "I'm going to lay it all at your door," he at last determined. "Make out you've been nagging me for the place, because you want to do it over. It's to be a birthday present for you, do you see? Actually, I mean. I'll have it put in your name, to do with as you please."

"Oh, how lovely!" The long sigh of her delight was contradicted by a faint line between her brows. "Only, of course—it would be yours, too? Even if it were in my name, I mean? That is—you'd come here just as much——"

He was puzzled. "Certainly I'd come here. I love this place. What do you mean? What do you suppose, I'd expect you to exile yourself here in solitude?"

She laughed at this, with almost too much gayety; raised her chin, and laughed again. "No, no, of course. That would be silly. I don't know what I was thinking of. I'm so unbusiness-like. Just for a moment, the idea of having it my property, separate from you— Well, I like to think that things belong to us both together." She looked pleadingly at him, inviting his indulgence for this idea.

He accorded it by a deprecatory shaking of the head; then addressed her, as a man is glad of the opportunity for addressing a woman, with an adult condescension. "The house in town, the Long Island house are technically mine. Did that ever enter your very charming but somewhat addled head? You manage to feel rather at home in them, don't you? I should expect the same hospitality from you." He frowned on her, with a pretense of intolerance.

"Of course," she murmured. "Then it's perfect." Her eyes were lowered in an apparent scrutiny of the pattern of the table-cloth. When she raised them, they appeared wide and dark in the pure pallor of her face. As though blindly, she fumbled on the table until her hand found Jay's. She gave a short, tender laugh that sounded like a sob.

ii

Outside the light was growing dim, and shadows began to gather in the corners of the room. The open door admitted the poignant scents of the spring evening. From the stove came a dull bubbling sound, and the sharp fragrance of coffee. The man and the woman sat very still, their hands lying quietly together on the coarse white cloth. The moment hung suspended, like the interruption of a quick rhythm.

Jay was the first to speak. "How about some coffee?"

"Of course, dear. I'll get it." Smoothing down her blue gingham apron, she rose. As the coffee boiled over with a soft commotion, she went briskly to the stove. Thriftily, as though enamored of her rôle, she wiped the side of the pot with a cloth, then enveloped the heated handle in its protecting folds. Her brow was puckered with thought, and suddenly she laughed.

"After all," she said, ruefully. "I'm just an ornament."

Jay was diverted from some preoccupation of his own. "You are, my dear. Though it might come more gracefully from some one else."

She surveyed the cups and saucers, selecting two with her free hand. "Economically speaking, darling! I'm the parasitic wife. I'm of not the slightest use." She sighed. "I'm happy to-night, pretending to be useful," she said, half to herself; and very dutiful, tossing her head, as though conscious that her blue gingham was becoming, she crossed the uneven boards of the kitchen floor to the china-scattered table beside the open door.

Her tongue's tip protruded ever so slightly between her lips as she deposited the precariously balanced cups. Intent on her task, she did not directly look at Jay, who sat heavily forward beside the table, eyes lowered, the inside of his upper lip lightly pinched between his teeth. His expression conveyed an absent-minded absorption in some train of thought; and, mechanically, as Lucia poured the dark, steaming tide of coffee, he clapped his hands to his pockets. Then his fingers obscurely fumbled inside his coat; rested, a moment later, on the edge of the table.

She set his cup before him, her hand almost brushing his. He was engaged in opening the cigarette case he had taken from an inside pocket. With a brusque, accelerated movement, he now scrambled out a cigarette, and dropped the case into the pocket of his coat. His wife had turned away. Covertly he scrutinized her profile with a sharp flash of the eyes. At once he was lighting a match, his long hands guarding the flame before his mouth.

Her own cup was unfilled. "There you are!" she cried, taking a spoon from the glass holder. "Now, let's see." She paused, staring at the table. "Oh, there's no sugar! *What* a mistake! Fancy giving you no sugar! You wouldn't have liked that." She almost ran for the balloon-shaped glass bowl. "Only granulated," she explained, rather breathlessly, as she set it before him. "But this is country style. And what difference does it make, anyway? Lump sugar is neater, I could never see any other advantage." Her fingers moved across her throat, twitching the neck of her dress. She went toward the door. "Ah, what a lovely evening," she said, speaking in a small voice, as though she were trying not to gasp for breath. "The most perfect hour, I think. The lilacs are so sweet. I think I'll bring in a few." She looked with a startled movement of the head at her husband, who raised his coffee cup to his lips. "Before it gets dark," she murmured. "I think I'll just gather a few lilacs." With slow, casual steps, she passed through the door.

Suddenly she began to run. In the dusk she plunged through the pleasant close of apple trees, past the thickest clump of lilac bushes. There she sank to the damp earth, and crouched heavily forward, her arms clasped across her waist, like one who has been stabbed in the bowels. The heavy smell of the flowers floated about her. It was a sickening smell. She recognized that she felt sick. From what her trouble derived, she was not yet consciously aware. She knew only that it was disaster to have seen in Jay's fingers a gay Roman cigarette case, on which an elegant lady coquetted with her fan.

iii

The blood rushed loudly in her ears, and her heart seemed to spend itself in a wild, painful knocking. She was torn by her heavy, articulate breathing. Yet these rhythmic, hoarse sounds which racked her throat seemed remote and impersonal. Through the confusion of her distress, some corner of her mind listened almost curiously. Oh, my *God*. Oh, my *God*. The first two words came faint and strangled on the inhalation; the last rasped her chest on the exhalation, like a bitter cough.

Before her eyes was the image of the farmhouse room, bright and awful as an explosion. She could see every detail with too much vividness, a too brilliant reality. She closed her eyes, and the scene **of** that arrested instant seemed burned with acid inside her eyelids. The table with its coarse white cloth, the remains of their meal, the two clean white cups and saucers, the turquoise enamel of the coffee pot; her hands; Jay's hands; the glimpse of the cigarette case—all these things seemed to flare with a pitiless distinctness, a sharpness of realization not common to ordinary perception, as though the pearly dusk of the kitchen doorway had been cleft by a flash of lightning.

With an exquisitely heightened sensibility, she could apprehend the physical sensations of that moment, the tension of her arm as she lowered the coffee pot, the very swerve of her eyeballs, the cold smooth surface of the spoon. Then came that endless trip across the kitchen for the balloon-shaped sugar bowl, whose cut-glass surface abraded her fingers. Still crouching under the lilacs, she rehearsed the ordeal, as a spent runner might be haunted by the pains of his course. What did it mean, what did it mean? She shuddered away from the processes of thought. With characteristic self-protectiveness, she did not want to think. But thought returned, like the raw ache of pain, after the first numbness of a blow.

He is sleeping with her! she cried. She was deafened by her own whisper. And she fought to deny the unendurable truth of her words. It couldn't be, couldn't be. She had had only the merest glimpse of the cigarette case. She might have been mistaken. But she shook her head, making a wild sound, like a laugh. Then her throat rasped coarsely, as a man's does before he spits. Sleeping with her, she said again. She took a savage pleasure in using a vulgar phrase. They are having an affair—ack no! A less common expression condoned it.

He went to her today, today. Her voice was monotonous, high, inhuman, as it quavered the words, repeating them as though determined to flay herself with the truth. He went to her today. *My* day. Our anniversary. He went to her on our anniversary.

iv

She began to run wildly in the direction of the road. The branch of a tree slapped her cheek. She stumbled; lunged frantically on over the uneven ground. I'll run away, she gasped, right now I'll run away, down the road. I don't care where I go. What does it matter what becomes of me? This isn't the first time. He thinks I never guessed. He thinks I'm a fool. I'll run all night. I'll fall down and die of exhaustion. I'll do anything before I'll go back. He thinks I never suspect anything. When he hasn't made love to me in two months! I won't be under the same roof with him. He isn't fit to have a decent woman under the same roof with him. Never, never again—never—the same roof with him. . . .

She tripped over the roots of a tree and heavily fell. The physical shock and hurt were grateful, and for a moment she lay panting, her face on the ground, the smell of grass and damp earth in her nostrils. Her reserved and fastidious nature was outraged by the primitive force of her passion. Yet in this sweeping away of all reasonable barriers and restraints, there was a kind of mad freedom. She had burst through decorous limitations, and was liberated in an ecstasy of suffering. She felt that she could express herself only in some desperate act; and the name of Hallie Ennes pierced her side like a white-hot knife. With a fierce satisfaction at her own madness, she longed to kill the other woman, to kill herself in a burning need to slake her pain. Yet perhaps—she considered it—it would be a refinement of cruelty to let Hallie Ennes live. She would kill only herself. Then they would have something to remember in their long, wakeful nights together. Something else to think about, something else than each other. A woman with bedsprings in her voice. . . . By God, she would give them something else to think about.

Something else to think about! She sobbed the words, without tears. Now she lay limply on the ground, uncontrollably trembling. She no longer thought of running along the road until she dropped of exhaustion. She was possessed by a nauseous self-disgust. I might better be dead than trying to get even—like a waitress—she whimpered. I'll kill myself, I'll kill myself, that's the only dignified thing left for me to do. . . . But this fresh spurt of passion died in contempt for her concern with her own dignity. She stumbled to her feet, and raised shaking fingers to smooth her hair.

v

In the gathering dusk she became aware of a light among the trees on a rise of ground. It came from the kitchen of the Pardee cottage. Mechanically she began to ascend the gradual slope, as though drawn by the warmth of the golden light. She climbed slowly and difficultly, her legs almost failing under her. Leaning against the side of the house, she peeped through the window. By the kitchen table Marie Pardee stood, kneading a mass of dough. Her hands moved competently in the sticky paste. The mellow lamplight shone on her calm face.

For a long moment Lucia gazed at her, beginning to breathe more slowly. Once more she smoothed her hair. She felt weak and confused, like a person who has just come out of a delirium. As she hesitantly stepped toward the back door of the cottage, she heard from the road the noise of a motor. A horn loudly sounded. She paused. Below, on the driveway of the Farm, the long glare of headlights illumined the dark. Some one was coming to the house!

She had shrunk from the idea of returning to Jay, but now she began uncertainly to pick her way across the top of the slope. The idea of visitors braced her at once; gave her strength to summon self-control. But, more than this, the arrival of visitors meant deliverance. Obscurely, it seemed to break the spell under which she and Jay were hideously bound here; seemed to make possible a release from the torment of longer remaining. Sparing herself no bitterness of humiliation, Lucia confessed that she had schemed to get her husband alone with her this week-end, in the hope of arousing his love. With a numb, bleak sense of failure, she acknowledged her defeat. She had not been able to hold him, even for this single day.

She had, she drearily acknowledged, chosen the course of self-deception. Instinctively feeling that suspicion was vulgar, she had refused to admit the evidence of her observations, of Jay's altered behavior. But now she could no longer close her eyes to the truth. He was infatuated with a strange woman whom no one knew anything about. Cut flowers, he had called such women. He had chosen a pretty phrase. . . . There was no passion left in her; only an emptiness, a despair. Her arms hung heavy from her shoulders.

It was amazing, incredible that such things could happen. Her husband had been the heart and center of her life, possessed of her confiding and intimate love. Now she could barely remember his face.

He had become unimportant. In that first stran-
gling outburst under the lilac bushes, all emotion
had died in her.

To the woman, standing alone on the hill in the
falling night, her life seemed like a dish which has
been cooked without salt. She turned from the
thought of it with a bitter indifference. But remembering that she had explained her husband's
coldness as the result of nervous strain and anxiety,
she was overwhelmed with self-pity. Her lips loos-
ened, as though a shir-string had been pulled out,
and her mouth filled with water. He had allowed
her to worry about him, to yearn over him, to show
him consideration. At the moment, this thought
bruised her more than all the rest.

She was standing at some distance from the Pardee cottage, at the spot where the rise of ground
sloped obliquely to the Farm. Now she could see, in
the pale shafts of the headlights, the dim rectangle
of the doorway, half hidden in trees. A figure, thin
and erect like Randolph, crossed the front of the car.
She was moved to a renewed hope of escape, which
set her heart fluttering; and, clasping her hands over
her breast, she told herself that she must be calm.
She would be able to get away. Beyond that, she
dared not think.

vi

Her eyes strained through the semi-darkness, as
though she were seeking for inspiration in the scene.

She must get away; but she must not betray herself. How was she to do it? She was conscious of a dull pain in her ankle; evidently, in falling, she had turned it. If she were to hurt it badly? They would have to return to town, or at least to Paula's; a severely sprained ankle would require a doctor's attention. She might, she reasoned, fling herself down this rock-strewn slope; in the dusk she would be sure to trip and heavily fall. That would do; it was not ingenious, but it would do.

She stepped irresolutely forward, skirting a clump of bushes. Not far below she discerned a pale, squarish shape. She peered at it, perplexed, until she recalled that on this elevation of ground at the side of the main house stood the tank which held the water supply.

She drew a long breath. It was settled, then. She did not consciously plan. She scarcely hurried. It had all been so perfectly revealed. She crept to the tank, and felt her way along its cold side. At the end, stooping down, she fumbled for the tap. It was stiff, and at first resisted her straining fingers. Kneeling beside it, she strove with both hands until it suddenly yielded. A heavy stream of water gushed with a rushing noise to the ground.

For a moment she stood, looking toward the house. Then she walked down, past the dark masses of the lilac bushes. Suddenly she turned and began to tear at the bushes. Her arms filled with scented branches, she ran like a cat to the kitchen door.

As though fearful of the reception she might meet, she paused. Jay was lighting a lamp. He had removed the shade and the chimney, and was engaged in adjusting the wick, while the bright jet of the match waited, trembling lightly, in his nervous fingers. With a kind of fascination, Lucia watched the match touch the wick. Then the chimney was fitted down, and the wick became a serene coronet of fire.

Her eyes moved with apprehension to the clock, which the glow from the lamp illumined. She had been gone just twenty minutes.

vii

Randolph leaned familiarly against the rocking chair, where Emmy sprawled, her slim legs outstretched. "You have callers," he informed his sister.

She went to the table and dropped the great bunch of lilacs; her eyes rested on the flowers. "How lovely!" she said. "How nice of you to come. Look at my lilacs, aren't they beautiful?"

"Lucy, what have you been doing?" Jay asked. In his amused, tolerant tone, it might be read that no anxiety was associated with her absence from the room. "I thought perhaps you'd gone to see the Pardee family."

She had lowered her face to the flowers, seemed to breathe their fragrance. "No, no. I didn't go in. I just took a little walk. It was so lovely, I couldn't come back at once. And the lilacs tempted me. On every bush I seemed to see lovelier ones. The illusion of the dusk, I suppose." She spoke with animation, breaking off with an excited little laugh. "Oh, it's too beautiful, too wonderful, in the country when night is falling." She turned to Emmy, her eyes very wide and bright. "Don't you think so, don't you know what I mean?"

"Yes," said Emmy vaguely. "Yes, it is beautiful."

Lucia sat down in a chair near Emmy. She smiled vividly at her, raised her eyes to Randolph's face, which wore a skeptical frown. "Look at him!" she cried, laughing uneasily. "Look how Ran's staring at me. So disapproving. Brothers are dreadful. Have you ever had a brother?" she demanded of Emmy. "It's all right for other women to be temperamental, they find it amusing and splendid. But a sister! Never! See, Ran, I'm a dryad, or something, like one of Penelope's poems. See, my hair is coming down." She twisted a dark strand about her fingers, laughing again.

"The lady," said Jay, "is mad." He had again taken out his pipe. After lighting it, with that air of intense absorption peculiar to the performance, he bent over Lucia with a pretense of concern. "The most quiet and well-behaved of wives until this moment, I assure you," he told Emmy.

"Ah, we aren't supposed to have separate lives of our own, you know." Lucia rose, with a slight contraction of the shoulders. "We wives. We're only of importance in our relation to the husbands. We aren't allowed, for example, to be unusual. That's queer. People would talk. It would reflect discredit on the husbands." She went to the table, where she lingered, picking up a crust of bread, putting the lid on the sugar-bowl. Her eyes avoided her husband.

Randolph looked down at Emmy, shaking his head. "She's scarcely noticed us," he said. "My poor little mouse of a sister! And we thought she'd make such a fuss. She isn't even surprised. She hasn't even asked us why we came."

Lucia raised her head, arrested. "Why did you come?" For the first time, it seemed to occur to her that their arrival had not been expected. "That's so. Why did you come?"

"We came to bring you back," Emmy explained. "They've planned the most priceless party. Paula said she couldn't bear to have you miss it. It's to be a treasure hunt. You know, every one puts up some money, and they hide clues in all sorts of out-of-the-way places. And the first people to find all the clues are the winners and get the money. Oh, you'd better come! It isn't so far, you know. You needn't stay late."

"A treasure hunt! What a good idea!" Lucia

exclaimed. "Oh, I do think treasure hunts are great fun."

Randolph sank into the chair his sister had left. "Well," he said, and he threw out his hands in a gesture of astonishment, "I expected almost any reaction from you—except that particular one."

In the doorway, Jay slowly smiled. "Apparently, my dear," he said, "they came simply to annoy us. They didn't think we'd want them. They were sure we wouldn't go back to Paula's. But still they came."

Randolph addressed Emmy softly. "How self-centered people are! Actually, it interferes with their perceptions. If you must have the truth," he told his brother-in-law, "we were fed up with that noisy crowd. We seized the first opportunity of dashing into the night. Dinnerless. Didn't we?" He laid his hand over Emmy's slender fingers.

"You see how fearfully we wanted your company," she murmured to Lucia.

But "Nonsense!" Ran reproved her. "Why pretend? We didn't care a brass hat-check for their company. We came for the ride!"

viii

Releasing Emmy's fingers he rose, made the suggestion that they must be starting. With sudden agitation, his sister moved to detain him. "Of

course you won't!" she cried. "You mustn't, you
can't go yet! Why, you—you haven't had dinner.
I'm going to get you some. Emmy looks half-
starved." Impulsively, she put her arm around the
girl, persuaded her to remove her small hat of green
felt. "There's plenty to eat," she said pleadingly.
"I can warm it up in a second. Do you see, Jay and
I didn't eat half the steak. Marie Pardee has old
pioneer ideas about food. Though Ed doesn't look
much like a barbecue, does he?" She pulled ener-
getically at the shoulders of Ran's coat. "Come,
my darling brother. I'll have a simple country re-
past for you both. Ready almost at once! Emmy,
help me clear the table, will you?"

"I'd love it," Emmy admitted. She clasped her
hands, rapidly blinking her eyes. It might have
been guessed that she was a little girl at a party.
She gayly accepted the apron which Lucia fetched
for her. "Look, Ranny, isn't it a blue duck?" she
exclaimed, and she smiled widely, moving her shoulders and wrinkling her nose. "Where shall I begin?" she demanded of Lucia, who had gone to the
stove.

The older woman hesitated. "You might bring
me the coffee pot," she suddenly said. "I'll take my
coffee with you and Ran," she told the girl. "This
great urge for nature came over me before I had
any. I—I'll just fill the pot now, before I do anything else." She emptied the coffee and grounds;

measured a fresh allowance of coffee; and, abruptly, with a curious intensity in her face, she turned the tap above the sink. Water slowly poured into the blue enamel pot. When it was filled, she set it on the side of the stove, looking back at the thin stream of water which continued to run from the tap. She was still staring at it when Emmy, laden with dishes, interrupted her.

"I say, what a shame! You've wet those lovely shoes, walking in the grass. Oh, I'm afraid they're quite spoiled."

ix

Prettily, her taffy-blonde head tilted, Emmy set the table. She walked about the kitchen with a boyish stride, her hands deep in her apron pockets. Outside, under the apple trees, Jay and Randolph smoked and talked. Lucia seemed to work with a feverish energy, yet a quarter of an hour passed before she called Randolph to the freshly spread table.

Once more she raised the blue enamel coffee pot; she filled the thick white cups. "There!" she said. "Isn't this better than waiting till you get to Paula's?" Jay had sat down at the table with Randolph and Emmy and, taking her coffee cup, she moved to a chair at some distance from the others. She quickly swallowed several sips of coffee. In her manner some discomfort was apparent, as though she flinched under the occasional glances which her husband gave her. At length she rose and went to the angle of the room where the stove and sink were situated. Here she could not be seen by the three who chatted in the warm glow of the lamplight. The murmur of their talk, the faint clash of the silver and dishes came to her ears, as she stood beside the sink. Again, with that curious breathless concentration, she raised her fingers to the tap. A small trickle of water came. A chair squeaked brusquely on the floor, and in a panic she turned off the water. It was Jay. She did not look at him. She bent over the sink, scraping the dinner dishes.

His voice was low. "Lucy, look here, my dear. There isn't any question—you don't want to go back to Paula's?"

"Well, of course, you know how I feel!" She rattled the plates loudly, her head still lowered. "But naturally, if you'd rather go—really, I'm perfectly willing——"

There was relief in his voice. "Absolutely not. I don't want to go. I was about to ask you, even if you thought of going, to give it up. As a favor to me." He waited, but she did not reply. "That's fine, then," he at last murmured. and went back to the table.

She raised her clenched fingers to her mouth. Weakly, she leaned against the sink, while her shoulders shook with silly, spasmodic laughter. Then, once more, her teeth painfully pressed into her lower

lip, she reached for the tap. She turned it on full.
No water came.

x

For a moment, she clattered the dishes with shaking hands. Then, "Jay!" she called. "Come here,
will you? Isn't this rather funny? There's no
water. I got some for the fresh coffee a while ago.
Now there's none at all."

She had stepped from the space beside the sink;
and, breathing quickly, she stood near the stairs,
while he tried the tap.

"That's odd," he commented, frowning. "Wait
a second, I'll see in the bathroom." He leaped up
the stairs; in a moment had returned, shaking his
head. "None there, either. I'm going up to have a
look at the tank." Randolph volunteered to produce a pocket flashlight from his car, and the two
men went out.

With their departure, a crazy activity possessed
Lucia. She darted giddily about the room, clearing
the table, setting back the chairs. Emmy's efforts
to help her she scarcely heeded. When order had
been restored, she took off her apron and hung it on
its peg. Her bright, dark eyes flickered to the doorway. As her husband entered, she looked at him
for the first time since she had returned to the house.
Her face was strained. There was no warmth, no
recognition in her gaze. Her husband might have

been a stranger from whom she expected important news.

"I don't understand it," he wearily said. "The tank's empty. I tried it with a stick. Not an inch of water."

Randolph went to his sister, shook her arm. "Now you'll have to come back with us," he told her. But her eyes were still coldly fastened on her husband's face. His brow was disturbed, his lips compressed. It was evident that a strong reluctance pervaded him.

"It won't be convenient," he murmured, "but we could make out, my dear." He gestured briefly to the pail beside the door. "I could bring up water from the lake. It wouldn't be so bad, you know. I've done it before." There was an appeal in his voice, his eyes, the droop of his shoulders.

But Lucia scarcely hesitated. She seemed to speak from some superficial layer of consciousness, beneath which nothing could pierce. "Well, my dear," she said in a deprecating, hopeless voice. And she gave another of her little laughs, a bursting bubble of sound, a punctuation mark made audible. "Really, I *don't* see— Wouldn't we be absurdly uncomfortable?"

He turned to Randolph, handing him the flashlight with a word of thanks. In him there was still discernible that curious, that uncharacteristic hesitancy. Yet, as once more he looked at his wife, he appeared to shake it off. He raised his chin with the familiar air of assurance; his shoulders straightened. So a man, caught without his armor, might quickly assume it.

"Is it actually worth while, I mean?" Lucia's shallow tones persisted. "Isn't it rather obstinate of us to persist in staying? We can come next weekend. Or the one after. What does it matter?" She turned away.

Jay nodded his head. "Very well, my dear." A slightly emphasized formality was the only token of his regret. "Naturally, we'll do as you wish. It's clear you don't want to stay." In a moment, he went on. "I'll have to speak to Ed. And see about locking up for the night. "I'll bring down the bags, and your things." He went quietly up the stairs.

Lucia's hand clutched the table edge. "I want to ride back with you," she suddenly told her brother. She looked toward Emmy, who was putting on her hat before the mirror. "Let me ride back with Ran," she said in a small, imperative voice. "I have something important to say to him, a family matter. Would you mind coming with Jay?"

"Why certainly not." Emmy's pink and white face looked with surprise out of the mirror. Almost at once she went on, "Of course that would be ripping." But her eyes darted regretfully to Randolph.

As Jay came down the stairs Lucia ran to seize her hat and coat. "I'm going ahead with Ran," she informed him. "You're going to have most charming company." She made a flippant gesture toward Emmy; and with a deliberate dignity as though calmed by the immediacy of escape she walked from the room.

xi

Randolph guided the car into the road. There it gathered speed carrying them swiftly through the dark countryside. As they gained a stretch of straight roadway he took one hand from the wheel and for a moment laid it on Lucia's.

"What's wrong?" he abruptly asked. "Your hands are cold. You're upset about something. I suppose you'll deny it. But what's the use? It's quite apparent."

"Why should I deny it?" She lightly deprecated the suggestion. "I *am* upset. Nothing serious, just nerves. It's too annoying. I'm ashamed of myself. I'm grateful to you for bringing me away," she assured him. "I know you and Emmy wanted to ride back together. I haven't anything to talk to you about. I just said that for an excuse." She twisted her fingers, evidently feeling some further explanation was necessary. Suddenly, "I couldn't stand it, Ran, I couldn't stand it. I couldn't wait for Jay. I had to start at once. It was a kind of impatience—

oh, that sounds such a little thing! But it over-whelmed me, it was like suffocation——"

"Your nerves, of course." He was gentle with her. "Have you felt that before?"

"Before?" She hesitated, laughed dryly. "Yes, I've felt it before. This was worse, more acute, that's all." She was impelled to talk, in a low monotonous voice which seemed to take no account of her listener. "I don't think we know ourselves. What's in us. We see only a little part. Like the headlights, which show a narrow track of road, a flash of fields and trees. The rest is blackness. In our minds, too, are all those hollows and forests and swamps, a wilderness that we don't guess." She shivered.

At last her brother answered. "I've never heard you speak so sincerely. You mean what you're saying. That's unusual for you. We're artificial creatures, all of us. But sometimes, at least, we lower the mask. You never do."

"I don't know what you mean!" she quickly pro-tested. "I've told you everything, I'm just nervous to-night——"

"I'm your brother!" he cried suddenly. There was an accent in his voice which she had never heard. "You don't care much about me, I know that. Archie was the one you were close to. Yet now, if you can't go to a friend, can't you talk to me? Can't we be honest with each other for once, Lucia?"

She straightened her shoulders fastidiously. "I do care for you," she said. "How absurd of you, Ran. What a silly thing to say. Really!" Yet, as though his appeal had weakened some barrier in her, she began again to talk, making a constrained attempt to be casual. "The fact is, I suppose, that I've wasted too much emotion on Nickie. Funny thing, being a mother! I've been so centered on him. Perhaps you don't realize. I suppose I haven't enough to give out in my other relationships." She paused, huddling under the rug from the chill of the night air. "Right now, I'm tormented by the thought that I've left him. It was selfish of me to think only of my own pleasure. I'm afraid he's been made unhappy. I blame myself for coming away."

Randolph did not reply, and unsteadily she went on. "Strange how we revert under the pressure of nerves or anxiety—emotion of any sort. We become quite banal, common, melodramatic. What does that mean, I wonder? Perhaps, just under our skins, we're actually like all the stupid people we affect to despise. Or perhaps the things we call stupid are merely the human, the universal things." Her strained voice dropped, and she tried to laugh. "Actually, don't you see—you can't pretend I'm so reserved, I'm spilling everything to you—I'm sitting here, thinking about my baby. I don't think of him as Nickie. I want the sentimental tag: my baby." Her voice broke. She was silent. With increasing speed, the car swerved through the night.

But I must go on living—for my baby! a voice within her cried. And, covering her face with her hands, she began to sob.

CHAPTER X

i

AMONG the trees hung Chinese lanterns, like glowing, imponderable fruits. Intermittently, from the house came music and the light chatter of voices. Lucia stood on the porch, waiting for Randolph to join her. As a whirl of laughter rose from the living room, she shivered and turned away.

Penelope's contralto baby tones came clearly through the closed door. "Of course I'm an orchid. Paula's a water lily. Green and white and cool. With soft, lonely leaves, floating——"

Paula shrieked. "But it's the oldest *rag!* Look how it's *torn*. Positively indecent. It's lucky I'm among *friends*."

Penelope pursued it. "What's Eva? Let's see, that misty azure chiffon. Mightn't Eva be a forget-me-not?"

Paula shrieked. "Oh, you can't call dear Eva a forget-me-not! It's quite too Victorian. Eva must be a sharper flower, something big and expensive, that hasn't any *smell*."

"No, no, please, Penelope!" came Eva's acrid tones. "Please, something else. Not a forget-me-not, not a sentimental flower, like a governess's valentine."

Randolph came up the steps of the porch. His hand on his sister's arm, he piloted her to the door. She began to wring her hands. "Why did I come here, why did I?" she moaned.

She found herself inside the house.

ii

At the foot of the stairs clustered that soft bouquet, Penelope, Paula and Eva. They brightly rushed to Lucia, laid delicate hands on her. Hearing the soprano confusion of greetings, Adrian came from the living room, handsome in his dinner clothes.

"Well, of course, I *told* you it was silly to *leave*. We're going to have the most marvelous treasure hunt——"

"Lucia, I'd have sworn you wouldn't come. Where's Jay?"

"Why, you sweet thing, what a happy surprise!"

"Hello, Lucia. Where's Jay?"

She looked hesitantly at Randolph, who still stood beside her. He addressed Paula, pirouetting on pale green satin toes. "I've been asked to announce that you've two more guests for the night. There's no water at the Farm. At least, there's a whole lake. But these are pallid, civilized folk. A lake doesn't interest them."

"Well, I don't wonder!" Paula was triumphant,

vindicated. Five sharp, shining finger-nails lay on Lucia's shoulder. "What did I *tell* you? I knew you wouldn't be *comfortable*. Look, aren't we gay? Did you see all the lanterns? Darling, admit this is more fun than the old Farm!"

Music again came from the living room. Lucia raised her hands to her flushed cheeks. "Of course, of course!" she cried. "It's quite wonderful. Marvelous. You're all looking very lovely. I wish I were dressed. What about the treasure hunt? Why don't we begin? I want to begin at once."

"But we can't begin until Jay and Emmy come," Paula protested. "Where did you leave them? Well, they'll be here in a minute, I suppose."

Her sister-in-law took off her small brown hat, pressed back the hair from her forehead. "Oh, no," she murmured. "That's true. We couldn't start without them."

iii

Adrian was inclined to raillery. "You've given up your honeymoon," he said. "Such a speedy disillusionment! Don't tell me you were bored—not a sweet, sentimental thing like you."

"It's the most cynical thing I ever heard of!" Eva exclaimed. "So much more bitter than never starting at all."

Paula twirled her green and white draperies. "But, you see, I *told* you that was Lucia's technique!

She just pretends to be sentimental. Of course, men would be taken in by it. But I'm surprised that you were, Eva!"

Lucia swayed, and Adrian put his arm around her. "You're tired," he discovered. "Come in and sit down. We'll find a nice corner, and I'll be very sweet to you. I feel as though I'd enjoy being sweet to you."

iv

Peopled with animated figures, in the glow of the shaded lamps, the high, white-walled room received a new semblance of frivolity, on which two austere family portraits looked disapprovingly down. Lucia's eyes, avoiding the crowd, moved to the sofa where that afternoon she had sat with Luis. He was again seated there, engaged in conversation with Revel. She observed, unable to recall if it had been true in the past, that he was one of those men to whom dinner clothes are unbecoming. The black and white made him look sallow, spare, though it lent him an air of sorry distinction.

She spoke softly to Adrian. "I want to sit over there." And greeting Revel and Luis, she sank on the sofa with a little sigh. Paula called for Revel, and he left the room. It seemed to Lucia to grow increasingly noisy. From the piano sounded a bright confusion of strangled rhythms. Several couples were dancing. Chatter rose in rapid gusts. She sat very still, looking down at her hands, which were folded on her lap.

Revel came back into the living room. His face looked worn. His eyes were very tired. Yet he turned without impatience to his wife's sharp questioning.

"Revel! Didn't you go—? I asked you to go see——"

"I did, Paula. She's quite all right. Sackett's sitting with her. She's finished dinner. They said they'd be right in."

Luis French sat in silence, a constrained smile under his small, stiff mustache. But Adrian was disposed to conversation. "—and I told Paula she's missing such an opportunity here. This room is charming, but quite wrong. A simpering hybrid room. Now just look under this covering—there's red plush, Lucia, I assure you, it's red plush. Can you imagine covering over anything so deliciously archaic as red plush?"

Some stir in the doorway made Lucia turn her head. Hallie Ennes had come into the room.

v

This woman, pale and slender, had been said to resemble Lucia; a stranger might have mistaken them for sisters, of different temperament and history. Each had a dark, smooth head, proudly

poised; each was slimly made, with narrow hands
and feet.

Sackett East accompanied Mrs. Ennes; and drawing her from the others, he led her to a deep chair,
and took a place at her side. She had a curious
gliding walk. On close inspection, the quality of
her resemblance to Lucia almost vanished. The
oval of face had a similar shape; but of Lucia's poignant delicacy, her mild reserve, distinction, languid
calm, there was no trace. The mouth was heart-
shaped, with a full, scarlet lower lip. The eyes were
heavy-lidded. The skin, especially on the shoulders
and arms, where it contrasted with the pure white
of her dress, had a golden tinge like a peach.

For some reason, this woman's entrance caused a
ripple of attention. Many people disputed her claim
to beauty, but all eyes turned to her. Clearly she
was accustomed to this tribute, was with a proud
assumption of disregard aware of it. She sat almost
disdainfully in the great chair, her breast raised, her
head inclined toward Sackett, while her eyes, mournful, unseeing, were fixed on the opposite wall. She
held a small carved powder box of white jade, which
her fingers restlessly opened and closed with a faint,
snapping sound.

Luis French had a light in his romantic eyes.
"Who is that woman?" he cried.

Adrian answered him. "That's Mrs. Ennes.
Supposed to be fatal. Isn't she a desperate, ripe, ex-

travagant creature?" he demanded of Lucia. "I
hear Jay's quite captivated," he went on. "But you
won't care! That's my quarrel with you, Lucia.
You're too calm, unmoved. It's superhuman of you.
Detestable. I'd rather you'd make a scene. Think
of the scenes Mrs. Ennes must have made! Can't
you see her? I can. Over anything. Over nothing. She has a vitality, that woman! It floats
from her in waves, like a heavy perfume. Sackett
shouldn't sit so near her. With that bad heart of
his! There, he's bowing his head. He'll faint, I
assure you Sackett is going to faint."

Luis continued to gaze at the woman. At inter-
vals, between the noise of conversation, her strange,
sweet voice could be heard. "She has the most tragic
face I've ever seen," he murmured.

At this Lucia's eyes flickered. Some attentiveness
seemed to pervade her; she turned to Luis with a
wide, intent, startled regard, like one awakened from
sleep. "You mean"—for an instant her glance
darted to Hallie Ennes—"you think she isn't
happy?"

"Desperately, passionately the reverse," he insisted.

Adrian laughed at her. "Come, Lucia, you can't
make me believe you don't see that. You're too
keen an observer. And every one knows she's had
some dreadful history. She married badly, I believe, when she was a young girl. She adored the

man, and he broke her heart, the usual story. Then
her child died. There's been much more since, I
imagine. It's all in her face."

She was suspended by this thought. At last she
said, "Yes, I suppose—it is. I hadn't considered—
hadn't really thought about it before. No, what
you say is true. She doesn't look happy. Strange
that a woman like that, whom every one admires—"
She broke off, as Penelope danced to the couch and
lightly knelt before them.

"You're talking about Hallie Ennes," she whispered. "Isn't she wonderful tonight? I never go
near her. She draws all the light in the room. She's
a golden woman. Penelope's silver. Lucia's silver,
too." Over her shoulder, she snatched an elfin peep.
"She wears her mouth like a bleeding heart," said
the poetess; and, sighing, she searched for her lip-
stick in a little beaded bag.

vi

To Sackett's evident discomfiture, Randolph now
stood by Mrs. Ennes's chair. Lucia observed them,
as she forced herself to rise from the sofa, to greet
the others.

"Why, good evening, Mrs. Ennes," she at last
said, her voice lifting, as though with pleasure and
surprise. Briefly she clasped the woman's fingers.
For a moment their eyes met. Hallie Ennes nodded

to Lucia, forcing a smile to her drooping mouth; but she did not speak.

As Lucia turned away, the outside door was heard to close, and Emmy came into the room. "My word!" she cried, pushing back her hair with a boyish gesture. "Weren't we quick? Jay drove like a demon." Her hands plunged in the pockets of her green tweed coat, she went to Randolph's side. Lucia moved to the end of the room, where the group clustered around the piano. She sat down in a chair, making herself very small, as though she wanted to remain unobserved. Again the outside door opened and closed. She rested her flushed cheek on her hand. She looked indifferently toward the door which opened on the hall.

Jay's entrance was deferred by the moment of his pause, in which he seemed, with that characteristic movement of the shoulders, to get his bearings in the room, relating it and its occupants to himself. An observer might have suspected a reluctance to enter. But hearing Paula's joyful shriek, he came quickly forward. His face was unsmiling, almost stern. He seemed possessed by a tense and resolute calm. He went to Hallie Ennes and took her hand.

From the corner where she sat, Lucia, by straining forward, could see Jay's face. The unaccustomed flush had suddenly left her cheeks. Her lips, faintly parted, were pale. Suddenly she bent her head, pressing the palms of her hands over her eyes, like a pitifully frightened child.

vii

Paula clapped her hands, demanding silence. "Come on! Let's get *started*. Sackett! All ready! Sackett's going to explain about the treasure hunt," she told them. "Oh, it's too marvelous! The treasure's a hundred dollars. Herman and Sackett made it up to that. Of course, we three can't any of us play, because we did the clues." With little imperative beckonings, she summoned them all to the center of the room. A roughly drawn map of the grounds stood on the mantel. "You can be studying that," she explained. She stood poised on pale-green toes, contemplating the map with her head atilt. "Herman made it, isn't it good? See, everything's there. This is the drive. The rose garden's over there. Up by the road's the barn. All this cloudy part is the Sound. Of course, this is the bathhouse. And the pier." A little wagging, pointing finger darted across the map.

Lucia had moved forward with the rest. Some instinct bade her protect herself by mingling with the others. Dimly she sensed that in a few moments they would all be expected to hurry into the grounds in pursuit of the clues which Paula had concealed. Doubtless they would search in pairs. Without turning her head, she knew that Jay still stood by Hallie Ennes's chair.

Paula was still talking, her tones rising shrilly above the murmur of voices. "Sackett's gone to get the first clue. While we're waiting for him, every-body choose a partner. Positively no wives and husbands together!" She shook her pert little head. "This isn't that *kind* of a party!" she said.

Lucia found that Luis French was at her side. "Will you be my partner?" he asked. "See, I went down to the village after dinner and bought a flashlight. I'm a very desirable partner."

She hesitated. "I'd love to be your partner, of course. But—I'm so tired. I don't think I'd be very good at anything tonight. Perhaps I'd better not." She was aware that Mrs. Ennes left the room. Jay stood looking about him; and, turning, she signaled to him.

"Ah, there you are! Where've you been? I couldn't see you anywhere. Good evening, Mr. French. Are you all right, my dear?" He solicitously regarded her face. "You're not too tired for this?"

Quickly smiling, she shook her head. "No, no. Why should I be tired?" The corners of her mouth seemed two pegs which tacked up a sagging fabric. With a painful intensity, her eyes followed Jay as he left the room. At the door, he was detained by Paula's cry of dismay.

"Jay! Where are you going? You come *back*, darling. You've got to be in the treasure hunt."

He reassured her. "I'll be in it, Paula. I'll be back in a moment."

Luis leaned close to Lucia. "Of course, if you're

tired, don't do it. I'll sit down with you somewhere, if I may——"

Her eyes were strangely bright. "After all," she said, "if every one's going to do it, I suppose it's foolish to be left out. I'm afraid I'd feel quite disappointed when I saw them all dashing off without me."

viii

"It's just like you," whispered Adrian, "to take another partner while I'm out of the room. It was quite understood between us. At least, I understood it. I'm sure I spoke of it to you. I just went on the porch for a moment with Penelope." He sighed. "I shall have to take her for my partner. A woman who's in love with Keats! That's worse than a husband."

Sackett, the picture of an orator, had taken his place before the mantel, and, tossing back his hair from his brow, he now began to explain the details of the treasure hunt. Six clues had been concealed about the grounds. Each clue, correctly interpreted, led the way to another. The first pair of players to discover the final clue would have earned the right to the treasure. While he talked, Paula distributed tags on which were to be pasted the small colored stickers which would be found with each clue. Thus, the winning pair must have on their tag six stickers of assorted shapes and colors.

Jay and Hallie Ennes were standing near the door. By slow degrees, Lucia edged nearer. "Let's not be too far away," she whispered to Luis. "If every one makes a rush for the door, we'll be left behind."

"I'm going to show you the first clue now," Sackett announced. He raised a square of cardboard to the mantel. In the instant before he turned it, Lucia gathered herself together, as a runner crouches before the pistol's crack. A low murmur ran through the group. "This is the first clue," Sackett repeated. Couples began to hurry, laughing, from the room.

"Come on, Lucia," Luis cried. He pulled at her hand. But now her tension was dissolved in reluctance. Jay and Hallie Ennes stood motionless, looking at the square of cardboard. Lucia suffered herself to be drawn into the hall.

"Wait a second," she begged her partner. "There's something in my shoe. Terribly sorry. Stupid of me."

Jay whispered to Hallie, and they made a dash for the porch. Lucia flung swiftly after them. Across the lawn in the darkness, she followed the flying wraith of a white dress.

ix

Below, on the terrace, which held the tennis court, was a bustle of movement, soft cries and laughter, the intermittent flashing of lights. Luis ran behind

her, caught her arm. "Here, Lucia, here," he said.
"The steps are this way. It must be the tennis
court. Don't you think? Look, there are your
brother and that blonde girl."

She was forced to stop. She faced him with reluctance. "The tennis court?" she stupidly murmured. "How do you mean?"

He explained. "Why, the verse—the first clue.
Something about a king holding court. It must be
the tennis court, don't you think? I couldn't make
anything else out of it. Could you?"

The white dress faded on the path which led
around the rose garden. Lucia put her hand to her
head. "Well, how stupid of me," she murmured.
"I suppose you're right. I wasn't thinking—" But,
resolutely, she gathered herself together. "That's
so obvious," she eagerly said. "Mightn't there be
some other court?" Again she looked in the direction where the white dress had vanished. "I know,
I know!" she cried, almost hysterically; and, seizing
her companion's arm, she began to run wildly toward
the path. Behind them, she could hear the expostu-
lations of Adrian and Penelope, coming without tri-
umph from the tennis court. "The badminton
court," she breathlessly explained. "It's back of
here, under the trees."

Before them, as they ran, glimmered a flash of
light. As they neared the trees, the white dress
moved from them, rushing toward the driveway.

"We must be quick," she gasped. She was trembling, as though under the strain of some dreadful excitement. "Randolph and Emmy will think of this. They'll see us. Here, where's your flash-light?" Taking it from his hand she threw swift flares over the court. At last they discovered a square of cardboard, fastened to a rustic bench; and, bending over it, they found a verse, and a box of star-shaped gold stickers. In their haste, the first players had overturned these on the grass.

Her breast rising and falling madly, Lucia strained her eyes to the legend on the card. Her lips moved, in a concentrated effort to understand the words. But she shook her head, wearily rubbing her hand across her eyes. She looked toward the path, hearing the light chime of Emmy's laughter.

"I don't know," Luis slowly said. "It might be an acrostic. The first initials of each line make B-A-R-N. Do you think that——?"

"Of course, of course," she cried. "Why didn't you say that sooner?" She dashed toward the road, running fleetly. "Come on," she called to Luis; but it was a perfunctory appeal, for her sudden spurt had taken him by surprise, and he was far behind. She gained the driveway; the smooth, firm track was grateful to her feet. Now, racing between the scattered globes of the lanterns, she gathered desperate speed. The white shape of the barn loomed through the darkness.

Again she saw a flash of light; and, crouching by the corner of the barn, she waited, spying at the wide doorway. Jay and Hallie Ennes came out, walking quickly, and in silence. She saw that they went down the drive, before she sprang into the barn. The flashlight was still in her hand, and by its light she soon found the square of cardboard. Mechanically securing a scarlet sticker, she mouthed the words of the verse written under the heading *Clue 3*. At once she sped to the door, tumbled into outstretched arms. Luis laughed.

"Have you found it? How fast you run!" In the soft spring night, he leaned against the side of the door, detaining her with caressing hands. She quivered restlessly, the light rhythm of her panting breath sounding through his words. "Catch your breath, dear! Ah, Lucia, it isn't worth it. You're tiring yourself. Let me see you." He took the flashlight from her listless fingers, and briefly illumined her face. His own showed dark and intense, yearning toward her. "Dear, you're lovely," he murmured, and he put his arms about her shoulders. "I'm troubled by you, by the scent of your hair. Like rose geranium leaves. Let me love you a little, Lucia. Let me give you a little happiness."

She broke indifferently away from his clasp; and with some fresh access of strength, stumbled down the drive. "There isn't time," she assured him. "I haven't time to listen. We must go on. See, the others are coming."

As they ran, three couples passed them, going in the direction of the barn. Ran and Emmy were in the lead. "I suppose you're right," Luis at last said in a dry voice. "You haven't time to listen. I shouldn't have spoken. I misunderstood."

x

"The clue is a famous president, something about a famous president," she told him. It was as though she had not heard him speak. "What could that be, Luis? A famous president? Let's see, Washington, Lincoln— Ah, I know!" She bounded forward, with a triumphant cry. "Sackett has a Lincoln car. Perhaps they've left it on the drive. Yes, there it is. I'm almost sure. Luis, quick, can you find the clue?"

Silently, he opened the door of the car, and examined the interior. Lucia strained forward, as though trying to pierce the darkness with her eyes. "Quick, Luis, quick," she implored him, clasping her hands. "Is it there?"

He held a cardboard square in his hands. "Here it is," he assured her, still speaking in a dry, constrained voice. "But I can't quite make it out. 'The clue is in arboreal tears.' That seems to be the key to it. A weeping willow, I suppose. Is there one on the place?"

Lucia's voice was dismayed. "There are three or four," she told him. "There's a big one," she went on, "down by the water, near the swamp grass. It's very conspicuous, perhaps they wouldn't choose it for that reason. Then—yes, there's another down there, too, not far behind the bath-house. We'll have to try there."

As they hurried past the house, shouts greeted them from the porch. Sackett and Herman Meyer stood on the steps, while Paula, wrapped in a light wool cape, perched on the railing. Lucia waved toward them, without pausing. She held Luis by the arm as they descended the steps to the terrace, where several misguided players still lingered, and began to run over the uneven ground below. Her eyes searched the darkness. It was very quiet. No voices sounded. Above the pier a light burned, but the intervening gloom was pierced only by the golden balls of a few Chinese lanterns.

Lucia wearily stumbled, stood still. "Have you any matches?" she asked Luis. He produced a box from his pocket, and she put out her hand. "Let me take them. Then we can separate, each take a tree. We'll save time. I don't need much light, I know the way better than you do. Now you'll find a willow over there"—she indicated a plumy shape against the gloom of the sky. "I'll meet you here," she cried, as she fled in the direction of the bath-house.

She searched under the giant willow, scanning its low branches in the tiny flames of the matches. There was no trace of a clue; and desperately she flung away from the tree, rushing in headlong search of Luis across the sloping ground. At once her heel twisted on a hillock of grass, wrenching her already weakened ankle, so that for a moment she stood still, clasping her foot in her hand. She called to Luis.

"Was it there?" she cried, as he came near. "Oh, I knew it wouldn't be! We made a mistake in coming down. All the rest are up above. We've quite lost the trail. Oh, why did I suggest this? It was stupid of me. We were so far ahead and now—" She put her foot to the ground, but raised it with an exclamation of pain. "I've wrenched my ankle," she told him. "It's nothing. But I won't be able to walk for a minute. Luis, you go on without me."

He repudiated this with indignation, solicitously putting an arm about her waist. "Naturally I won't. What do I care for this foolish game? I'm only in it because it lets me be with you."

"I'd really rather you'd go." She spoke in a dull, hopeless voice, staring down the sloping ground toward the water. In the glow of the light which burned above the pier, that long wooden track wavered with a ghostly gleam. The same light faintly illumined the ground adjacent to the bathhouse, and it was possible to distinguish a high hedge which bordered a square of grass. "I think, I'm almost sure, there's a bench inside that hedge. I could sit there for a moment." She still spoke in a weary voice, empty of resonance; and, leaning against Luis, she slowly limped down the slope. The low bench was readily discovered. She sank upon it with a long sigh. "It's useless," she went on, as if to herself. "We're out of it now. I can't go on."

He seated himself at her side, scanning her face in the half-light. He moved his shoulders in deprecation of her evident interest in the progress of the treasure hunt. "How I must bore you!" he bitterly commented, and turned away.

Again she did not seem to have heard. She gave a small cry, sharply started. "Luis!" she said. "Do you realize what it means, that light on the pier? They don't usually have it on—only when some one is bathing at night. Of course, don't you see, there's a clue hidden on the pier somewhere! Oh, I know it, I know I must be right," she vehemently insisted. In her excitement, she had taken his arm in both her hands. "They'd be afraid to have people going out on the pier in the dark. It's rickety, you know— holes between the planks."

To her this discovery was of evident importance; and, as though interpreting her companion's lack of response, she went on. "So you must go, Luis, you must find the other clues and come back for me. You can run. You won't mind?" she implored him. Turning, she glanced toward the dark slope of ground, above which gleamed the windows of the house. "You see, you see, no one is coming yet. We can get into it again. I'll be able to walk in a minute." Her impetuous hands almost pushed him from the bench, and he reluctantly rose.

"Very well," he said stiffly. "As you wish, of course."

"Go first to the willow to the right of the house— beyond the croquet lawn," she eagerly instructed him. Her eyes followed him as, tossing his dark head, he left the twilight area of the hedge.

xi

With his disappearance she fell forward, weakly, wearily. Her fingers touched and clasped her aching ankle. The night was cool and she spasmodically shivered in her light silk dress, which was wet with perspiration. The hedge near which she sat was spread with bathing suits, and the odor of damp wool mingled with the acrid scent of the water. Beyond its black expanse, she could dimly perceive golden pricks of light on the opposite shore. A small yacht was anchored beyond the pier, and the lights of other vessels clustered brightly here and there, below the scattered stars.

She was utterly alone, tired, chilled, in pain. Her exhaustion bowed her down, like a soft, smothering weight. Her neck felt limp and broken. It could scarcely support her drooping head. In her thighs and arms throbbed an intensity of fatigue scarcely less painful than her burning ankle.

The excitement which had sustained her at the
beginning of the treasure hunt was now quite vanished. Miserably she sensed the loneliness of the
night, silent save for the monotonous lapping of the
tide, high against the piles of the pier. She was
frustrated, defeated. In a dim effort to rationalize
her despair, she acknowledged that she had attached
an insane importance to her pursuit of Jay and the
woman. She had made their present escape the symbol of her greater, her complete disaster. With a
flash of hope, she turned her head. But no white
dress glimmered through the dark. She had lost
them irrevocably.

She pressed a cold palm against her brow, trying
to think clearly, calmly. What must it have been,
the story of Jay's relation with this woman? She
tried to remember, to imagine. But her mind was
dull and confused; her memories seemed worn and
thickened, like a pack of old cards. They must
have been lovers for two months. Two months.
Then last night at the Tailers' party, there had been
some trouble between them. People had noticed.
It had been quite apparent. They had gone into
the garden and, afterwards, the woman had looked
very white, very desperate. In the taxi-cab, going
home, she had spoken about it to Randolph. He
hadn't realized it was Jay. He wouldn't have spoken
about it, blurting it out in that hideous, laughing
way, if he had realized. . . .

xii

Lucia was shaken with a sick trembling as she huddled on the hard bench in the chilly night. She was beginning to work it out in her mind. For now she realized that the woman hadn't been able to bear the pain of the misunderstanding with Jay. She had telephoned him, demanded that he come to her. He had planned to be with his wife. They had arranged to go away together. But what of that? The wife was faithful, patient, considerate. Let her wait!

That woman well knew the strength of her hold on him. For he had responded to her appeal. He had gone. He had felt compunction, but he had gone. And he had not forgotten to ask for the cigarette case—that had made an impression on him! Unthinking, he had taken it out at dinner. For a moment he had held it in his fingers. It had betrayed him.

They had had a chance to make up their mis-understanding. Yet Jay had not wanted to come here to-night. So, curiously, he must have wanted to avoid Hallie Ennes. Perhaps he had divined that her power over him was fatal. Perhaps he knew himself so weak that he could not trust another meeting.

Where were they now? With this thought a new panic of fear awoke in Lucia's breast. She breathed in shallow gasps, moaning aloud. Where are they, where have they gone?

xiii

Her body, shivering in the cool air, seemed the very image of her stripped and defenseless spirit. She was beaten, broken. Pride was gone. Anger was gone. Only cringing fear remained.

She had torn down all her careful structure of sentiment and falsehood; had consciously acknowledged her husband's offense. To her gentle, evasive, romantic nature, the admission seemed, of itself, an additional misfortune; it racked her with a fresh despair. Above the confusion of her pain, her mind was swiftly weaving. She recalled with irony the numbness which had succeeded her outburst at the Farm. Then she had believed that all capacity for suffering had died in her. For Jay she had felt only an indifference. She had not been interested in him, had not cared to look at him. She had wanted only to get away, to escape. It had meant nothing that she was leading him back to Hallie Ennes. Her marriage was ended. With her husband's future she had been unconcerned. . . .

But he had come into Paula's living room, pausing for a moment at the door; looking around with that characteristic movement of his heavy shoulders. He had gone to the other woman. He had taken her hand. She, his wife, had watched him;

and, suddenly, her heart had gone liquid with fear. All her pride, all her strength, all the numbness of her indifference had been quenched by the dear habit of him. By the secure usualness of his fair well-brushed hair, the nervous movement of his hands, the clean white line of his collar, buttoning so neatly, so inevitably, on either side of his ruddy neck. Without him, all else was unspeakable, tasteless, unendurable. She could not live without him.

xiv

Resting one hand on the bench, she drew herself up and tried to put the injured foot on the ground. Little nerves of fire seemed to run from the ankle to her stomach. But, leaning low over the bench so that her weight fell heavily on her hand, she persisted.

They were very near before she knew that they were coming. As they passed the hedge, she heard the rhythm of their feet and the murmur of the woman's dress. She crouched low, half-kneeling on the bench. The hedge concealed her from their view.

They were moving down the straggling path to the uneven wooden incline which led to the bathhouse and pier. The woman walked ahead, and in the glare of light which shone above the pier, it was possible to see her dark, erect head, and the curious, swinging movement of her carriage.

At the top of the wooden incline, Jay paused. "Hallie!" he sharply called. "Hallie!" She turned, showed him the pale, ravaged oval of her face. "Let's go back to the house," he said. "This is absurd. Why are you doing this? Come, let's go back."

But she shook her head. She raised her husky, musical voice. "No, no. Let's go on. I want to find the treasure."

xv

On the dark slope of ground, voices sounded, lights flashed. Penelope gave a contralto cry. Adrian shouted a reply. But Ran and Emmy were the first to pass the hedge, running with arms entwined, shoulders touching. Slim and fleet, they cleared the wooden incline, and the boards of the pier rang under their springing feet.

Penelope followed closely, with Adrian in pursuit. Eva and Revel were left behind. They went down the last paces of the path at a jog-trot. "Oh, youth, youth!" Eva gasped. "Isn't it beautiful? It always finds the treasure," she said sadly to Revel. "I think I'll have a cigarette."

With a strange lightness and clarity, the voices floated back across the water: Emmy's girlish tones, Hallie's musical murmur, Randolph's laugh like a pleasant whinny. They were all rushing madly along the pier, eagerly trying to outdo one another in the discovery of the treasure. As Eva and Revel joined them, their wild hilarity increased.

Lucia rose carefully to her feet. Moved by the excitement on the pier, she found it possible to stand, even to take a few steps. She could see the pier quite clearly. The end was almost lost in obscurity, but she could discern Emmy's slender figure, as she moved about, throwing her flashlight over the edge. Emmy called, and Hallie's voice answered her, muffled, indistinguishable. It seemed to come from a spot beyond the end of the pier, where the float was moored. Jay and Randolph were separately searching under the flooring, kneeling to examine the tops of the supporting piles.

To Lucia, standing alone in the darkness, it seemed that the faint, uneven ripple of talk served only to isolate her further. The others were self-sufficient, oblivious of her. She watched their dancing flashlights. She shivered, feeling the night cling closely about her like a moist, black bandage.

She had ceased to expect Luis. She no longer thought of participation in the treasure hunt. Now she could at least see Jay, kneeling on the pier. With an absorbed attention, she watched his quick gestures, saw him rise and move on, and kneel to search again.

A triumphant cry sounded lightly across the water. "I have it, I have it!" Emmy's voice fluted, that sweet voice that had sounded over so many footlights. She was sitting almost at the end of the pier, and she waved wildly to Randolph, who hastened back to her.

"Good girl," he cried, as he ran, his feet making a hollow sound on the wood. "Good for you, darling!" He knelt at her side, bending low. From their dimly seen positions Lucia could divine that the final clue had been fastened to one of the piles, just underneath the pier. "Yes, we have it," Randolph called out. "It's down here, tied with a rope." There was a loud rumbling noise as the others ran to the end. Voices mingled.

"Emmy, you're wonderful——"

"Ah, youth always finds the treasure—and youth doesn't need it——"

"You were so quiet out here, we might have known——"

"Hallie!" Emmy's clear voice called. There was a pause. "Hallie!" Suddenly there was silence on the pier. "Hallie!" There was tension, the shade of a scream in her emotional young voice.

Jay's voice now took it up. "Hallie!" he shouted, bending over the end of the pier. And again and again, hoarsely, with an undertone of panic, "Hallie, Hallie! where are you?"

They flashed their lights, moving abruptly, with an altered tempo.

"There's a boat down there——"

"She was there a moment ago, on the float——"

"I saw her when I came out, she must be there——"

Then, across the water, strained and unfamiliar, Jay's voice sounded. "She's gone back to the house. She must have gone back. Eva, you and Revel must have seen her. Didn't you see her? Revel, you saw her?"

Their reply was inaudible. Emmy wailed. "She couldn't have gone back! She couldn't have, Jay, she couldn't have! I was right here all the time. Right beside the ladder. I'd have seen her——"

Penelope gave a little scream. Emmy began to sob. The men's voices were harsh and curt. They were forcing the women back from the end of the pier. "Here, bring your flashlights down on the float," Randolph shouted. "Hold them over the water." He flung off his coat, and went down the ladder.

In the faint light Jay appeared, coatless. He mounted the diving board. The white blur of his shirt described an arc. There was a heavy splash.

xvi

Alone beside the hedge, Lucia covered her face with her hands. She heard the cries of the women, running to the house to tell the others. But she did not call to them, did not move.

He has followed her even there, even into the water, she sobbed. And, beginning to wring her hands wildly, she thought how dark it was, how the tide was running out.   It was treacherous, the pull of the tide.

Jay, she screamed, my darling, come back to me, don't go any farther, come back, come back.

She was dizzy and faint and she let her weight rest on her injured foot, feeling the pain brace and distract her.   Jay, Jay, she kept crying, in a little chirping voice, swelling and fluttering in her throat like a frightened bird. . . . Jay, Jay, don't go, come back, come back!

CHAPTER XI

i

Lucia lay across the foot of the wide bed, waiting for Jay to come upstairs. He would soon come, they had assured her. He was quite all right; he had changed his clothes, and was none the worse for his plunge. Mrs. Ennes was all right, too. Oh, quite! They had all been very soothing. Now, Lucia, dear, don't ask any more questions tonight. . . .

They had put her in the best spare bedroom. It was a pretty room, with a bath of its own. Some one must have given it up to her. She wondered who. The bed on which she lay was a mahogany four-poster, with a canopy of pure, pale blue. She lay looking up at it, with wide eyes, as though it had been a summer sky.

She thought that she must have fainted. She could not clearly remember what had happened, after she saw Jay dive from the spring-board on the pier. The events which preceded that were misty, too. . . .

It was almost as though she had fallen asleep, and had awakened to find Luis bending over her.

She had been lying in the damp grass beside the hedge. He was rubbing her wrists, stroking her face.

There had come a vague interval, after which Adrian was there, too, standing by the hedge. Luis had been arranging how they should carry her to the house. But Adrian silently took her in his strong arms, and went striding up the dark slope. They moved quickly over the uneven ground; past the tennis court, past the absurd yellow globes of the Chinese lanterns. From the hall, she had seen Sackett lying prone on the long sofa in the living room, his face buried in the pillows.

ii

Paula had run in and out, executive. Paula blossomed in a crisis. She liked to take command, give orders. At once she had arranged for Lucia to be carried to the best spare bedroom. She had sent for her sister-in-law's dressing case, had seen that she was undressed and made comfortable. Some one had bound her ankle securely. Some one had pressed a glass of brandy to her lips.

They had been kind, very kind. But she had wanted them to go away. Just for a moment, she had wanted to be alone with Randolph. He had not been soothing, had not said she must not worry herself with questions to-night. Randolph had not pretended that Mrs. Ennes was all right. So that when he told her that Jay was quite well and would be up in a little while, she had been reassured.

He had bent over her, kissed her cheek; and she had felt how cold his lips were. She had seen how he was shivering, little muscles twitching about his mouth and chin. He had drawn on a pair of dry trousers and an overcoat, but his undershirt was soaking wet. She had made him promise to take a hot bath and drink some brandy.

Now she was alone in the pretty room, waiting for Jay to come up. She was confused and tranquil, staring at the pale blue silk of the canopy. The brandy might cause this.

iii

She had been utterly unfair toward Randolph. This thought clearly escaped from the haze in her mind. The fact was that she had never forgiven Ran because he would not live with Mamma. She had taken a highly moral attitude about it, censuring her brother for selfishness. This had been false. Highly moral attitudes were usually false. Of course, it had been a question of her own selfishness, not Ran's. She had been antagonistic to him because, through his defection, Mamma had been wholly thrown on her, the daughter, the mother's natural confidante and companion. She had expected to escape from Mamma when she married. It had proved to be a very incomplete escape.

Yet, living alone, Mamma had done quite well—
for Mamma. She had learned to expect less of
her children. If Randolph had stayed with her,
she would have nagged him to death. She would
have wrapped soft, detaining tentacles around her
baby. She had felt an advantage over him, because
he was her baby, because he had been delicate as
a boy, because he was affectionate and easy-going
and disliked unpleasantness in personal relations.

Now Mamma was growing old; she was not
strong. She could not always live alone. There
was no evading the fact that before so very long
she would have to share her daughter's home. The
realization of this had poisoned Lucia's affection for
Randolph, had constantly irritated her into petty
resentments. To others, to Ran himself, it must
have been apparent that she was ready to criticize
him on the slightest pretext, making the most of his
affectations and absurdities. But he had always
been good-humored, affectionate, uncomplaining.
She saw now that he must have loved her very
much, to have put up with her for so long. And,
oddly, she had loved him, too. That had added
bitterness to her annoyance with him; because she
had been angry at herself, had wanted to let herself
be fond of him. But she had started off on the
wrong foot, and she had had to go on being superior,
censorious. She had dramatized their relationship
to herself; the wise older sister and the foolish,

selfish young brother. Human beings did a great deal of this sort of thing. . . .

iv

Lucia raised herself on one elbow, and looked around the room. She was not so drowsy now. A light burned on the small table beside the bed on which she lay. She was covered with a silk quilt, pale blue like the canopy.

She wanted, for once in her life, to think everything through. There were other things, many of them, about which she had never been clear. They flitted, pale, elusive moths, through her mind. She must not try to hurry herself, get excited over them. If she remained calm, perhaps they would come of themselves.

Her dressing case lay on a chair. On the floor was Jay's bag. Jay would be coming up soon. She must wash her face, arrange her hair. Besides, she did not want him to find her in bed. He might think it was a strange thing that she should be resting comfortably in bed. It might seem to him that she was heartless and indifferent.

She rested her injured foot on the floor. Now that it was so tightly bound, it was possible to step on it, difficultly, but without great pain. She sat down on the broad couch, which had been made up for Jay to sleep on.

What sort of woman was she? She had always

been of analytical habit, yet in understanding herself she had signally failed. There had been too many emotional barriers, too many buried fears and taboos. Above everything else, she had been resolved to keep undisturbed the smooth, formal surfaces of life. She had had a dread of violence, of unpleasantness, of disorder. She had kept her mind at peace by denying the presence, the possibility of these things.

Through this she had of necessity deceived herself, living in the sweet, insecure precinct of her own self-protection. For life held unpleasantness, held disorder. It was not possible always to disregard violence.

v

Already, as she wearily sat in the quiet, pretty bedroom, it was difficult to believe that she was the woman who had flung herself under the lilacs in an abandon of emotion. It was scarcely credible that in a torment of bitter jealousy she had hated her husband, hated the other woman. Her humiliation and rage had swept her out of herself, out of her neat ideas about the surfaces of life. That was because she desired her husband for herself, and another woman had been able to take him from her.

And almost as strange was that mood which had come after, the mood of abject and pitiful fear.

She had wildly followed her husband and the woman, fearful only that she might wholly lose him. If she could not have his love, she must at least have his physical presence, her position as his wife. For this she would have fallen on her knees, pleading, begging contemptibly.

Now she felt that these moods, the one of violent rage and the one of passionate fear, must have been possessed by two strange women, other than herself. She no longer felt the emotion which had shaken them. Yet both these women must be buried within her, part of her body, part of her spirit.

vi

The other woman, Hallie Ennes, she need no longer fear, and hatred, too, had vanished. She was shocked by the idea that she was dead, but it did not cause her pain. She had no emotion about her at all, except a dull feeling of disaster.

In her pain and disillusionment, in the drama of that headlong pursuit through the darkness, she had attached an insane importance to the part the other woman had played in her life. It was not only because Hallie Ennes was dead that Lucia now could think of her calmly. Suppose that Jay had had a passing physical infatuation for her? What of that? It could never have altered the stability of his marriage, of his life.

Lucia put her hand across her eyes. She had made one of her mistakes in failing to accept a rational conception of marriage. Intellectually she had acknowledged that a man is not satisfied with one woman; that the normal, imaginative male craves diversion, adventure, satisfaction of his curiosity. In the abstract, she would have been prepared to admit this; but, concretely, such ideas and experiences seemed to her vulgar, and always she had made an unconscious reservation in favor of Jay. To her *any man* had meant *any man but my husband*.

Yet she knew what manner of man her husband was, full-blooded, self-willed; she knew that he enjoyed the company of women. She had accepted the fact of his flirtations, refusing to be jealous of the many women who had figured lightly in his life, while she had closed her eyes to the inevitable implications.

Perhaps a woman of her gentle, sentimental nature would always be wounded by the proof of her husband's infidelity. Perhaps she could never attain a worldly, sophisticated viewpoint, like Eva and the others. Lucia rose to her feet with a little gesture of despair. No, she could not utterly change herself. She could not adopt an attitude of mind which seemed to her cheap, shallow. To accept Jay's infidelity with indifference, she must uproot her love for him. She must turn into a woman of stone; or, while preserving the outward amenities of their relationship, she must fill his place with a succession of lovers.

It could easily be arranged. Jay never interfered in her life, according her the same freedom of action that he demanded for himself. There would be no unpleasant scenes, no sordid or humiliating subterfuges. Money brightly gilded the details of a light love-affair. It could be done elegantly, with *chic*.

At this moment, she had two men to choose from. Either would, she supposed, be charming. One of them loved her or—perhaps a more desirable alternative—fancied for the moment that he did. She was a neglected wife; her husband did not desire her. But other men desired her. She might have the reassurance of kisses, of close embraces; the lovely, heart-warming reassurance of words.

In the mirror of the dressing table she saw the white misery of her face. And remembering Paula, seated beside Herman on the bench, with red lips lifted, she thrust out her arms in a passionate gesture of rejection. No, no, no! she cried. I can't do that, I can't! . . .

vii

At once she made an effort to regain her composure, so unexpectedly shaken. There were in her life elements of great and permanent happiness. Upon these she should fix her thoughts. Hysteria led to nothing; already tonight she had been de-

luded by its crazy suggestion that Jay might leave
her.

Nothing was, had ever been, more completely im-
probable! There was in his character, in his
attitude toward her, nothing which suggested muta-
tion. In the ten years of their marriage they had
become bound together—it was implicit in everything they said, in all the plans they made—by a
thousand subtle ties of habit, association, convenience, affection, appearances, shared possessions.

Jay was a man who prided himself on his reputation for soundness, stability, common sense. He
smiled his wise, old sea-lion's smile at the folly of
men less firmly grounded in sagacity and good
judgment. Imagine his having to explain to all
the gaping world that his head had been turned
by a woman! Imagine his going to Mamma, to
Aunt Geraldine, whose idol he was! . . . I'm leaving Lucia for another woman. I love her very
deeply. Lucia will give me a divorce. . . . It was
unthinkable. Lucia gave a wavering laugh. Even
if Jay were to fall madly in love, there would be
nothing he could do about it. She should have
recognized that all along. He would have to give
up a love-affair, or carry it on secretly. Any other
conduct would be inconsistent with his code, with
his traditions, with his practical good sense.

His conversation that very day had contained a
dozen suggestions of the permanence of their relation. She remembered their discussion of Revel's

predicament. They were going to work out some plan of keeping it from Paula. It might be difficult, but for Revel's sake it was necessary. . . .

Jay would, in the first place, buy the Farm. . . . Suddenly Lucia started. She threw back her head, raising her clasped hands to her mouth. Of course, of course! Why hadn't she thought of that before? For a moment, she recalled, the suggestion had frightened her; she had foolishly said that she would not want to go there without him. And he had answered her, half impatiently, as though irked by her silliness, that of course he would be staying there, too. The words had been slight. But there had been something in the implications of the homely little scene, something ordinary and sane and intimate which completed her reassurance. She had already been persuaded intellectually. Now conviction seemed to pour over her in a strong stream of consolation, of relief.

Of course, of course, he had never meant to leave her!

viii

A heavy step sounded in the hall, and she raised hasty fingers to her hair. There was powder on the dressing table; as she dipped the puff in the shallow dish, the door opened. She felt that she was trembling. She half-turned on the narrow bench before the dressing table, not directly looking at her husband.

"Oh," he said. "There you are. I thought perhaps you'd be asleep. They said you hurt your ankle. That's too bad. Is it feeling better?"

She rose then, caught the back of a chair, on which she leaned. "Yes," she said faintly, "it's better. Nothing serious. I turned it on something. Down by the bath-house."

He seemed to flinch. "Oh. You must have been down there then. For quite a time."

"Yes, quite a time. I fainted, I think." She fell silent on that.

"There's my bag." He touched it with his foot, seeming to regard it with surprise. He lifted it to a chair, and mechanically unfastened it. She watched his bent back, as he lifted one or two articles from the bag. He wore an old heavy overcoat.

Slowly she moved toward him. "You've changed your things," she said. She had reached his side. Timidly she put out her hand and touched his fingers. They were cold, but he was not shivering. "Are you all right? You aren't chilled? You mustn't take cold."

He turned his head away. "Yes, I changed," he told her. "I'm all right."

"You're tired," she faltered, "you must be worn out." Suddenly words burst from her, as though she were choking. "Jay, such a terrible thing. Such a dreadful thing to happen. Oh, I'm sorry, it must have been so—so shocking for you." She paused, her hand pressed to her mouth, as though frightened by her own speech.

At last, he turned toward her. His face was in color a strange, uneven mauve. It looked drawn and altered. The lips were bloodless. "Yes," he said. "Yes. Shocking." In a moment he quickly went on, as though relieved to speak. "Her foot must have slipped. I shouldn't have let her go down on the float. I can't think why I didn't stop her. We went out on the pier, you know. She was down the ladder almost at once. She said she'd be careful." He waited a moment, staring straight before him. "I noticed it was slippery. The water must have washed up over it at high tide. I can't help feeling it was my fault, don't you see? I should have made her come back. Her—her foot must have slipped. I can't help feeling responsible." He looked down, frowning in a puzzled, harassed way. Then he passed his hand over his face, with a gesture of inexpressible weariness. His voice was hoarse. "Lucy, Lucy, I'm so tired! I dived so often."

He had spoken like a child, and her face grew beautifully tender. "Yes, dear, I know you're tired. Come, take off your things. They've made up a bed for you on the couch. Come, dear."

But he did not notice her hand quivering on the sleeve of his coat. He moved uncertainly to the door. "I'm going out. I can't rest yet. I just wanted to see if you were all right. You'd better go to bed, my dear." At the door, he turned, trying to settle his shoulders with that characteristic movement. "I'll just have a smoke before I come up," he said, with an excellent imitation of his own voice and manner.

ix

She was gripped by a new convulsion of trembling. It appeared to her that there had been something hideous in the scene she had just experienced with her husband. Both had been suffering. Neither could admit it. So artificial was the relation between them that, rather than break down in her presence, rather than let her see his pain, he had stumbled out of the room. When she was asleep, he would return.

The woman sat alone in the quiet bedroom. For the first time, she had longed to have the smooth, formal surfaces of life disturbed. For the first time, she suffered because she had not been able to bare the festering, disastrous truth. What could there be between two people who never looked into each other's faces, who spent their lives in masquerade?

Strange she should think of this! Such preservance of the amenities had always seemed to her the supremely desirable course. Perhaps her perceptions had been altered in those moments in the lonely dusk at the Farm, when she had been delivered over to a primitive abandonment of suffering. Fantastically she thought of the dusk as slashed into gray ribbons by her passion. And though the memory of that violence was horrible, though that excess outraged her moderate nature, she was conscious of an obscure satisfaction that she had been capable of such release.

Her emotion had swept her over the high strong walls of reason and discipline. Whatever people might think, she was not a cold woman. She was sure of this now. She had somehow missed the trick of transmitting her warmth, of giving it out to others. All her life she had been in such fear, in such disgust of violence. In safe-guarding herself against it, she had protected herself from emotion, too. All the deep emotion which lay within her nature was like a lock with a lost key.

x

Lucia sat very still, her hands lying in her lap, with the palms turned upward. She was thinking that her husband would never leave her. She had received the perfect assurance of the permanence of their marriage. If he had not left her for this woman, he would never go. For now she knew how Hallie Ennes had been able to make him suffer.

She had had a power to disturb him, and she had not relinquished it. He had lost her in the strength of his desire, and her beautiful dead hands would draw and detain him. She would keep him longer than a living woman could ever do. Drearily, Lucia confessed that she would never be able to watch him tire of her; never know the satisfaction of seeing the affair tarnish, as the others had done. This woman's glamor could not fade, her beauty could never stale. He would always see her in the freshness of her arrested vitality, her interrupted loveliness.

And, thinking of the dead woman, Lucia no longer recalled that Jay had loved before; could no longer believe that he would love again. He was her husband; she possessed the habit of him, the prerogative of his name, the occupancy of his house. They were bound by association, convenience, affection, appearances, shared possessions. At night he would come home to her. He would go to bed in his room across the hall from her. She would administer his household, rear his child.

Such things gave her no command over his mind, his heart. These the dead woman might still retain. To win some part of them, she would have to scheme as best she might. She would have to do her best to interest him; dressing for him, undressing for him. There would be false starts, frustrations. Like the farce, the laughable failure, of this week-end trip, which she had planned for no other reason, for no other reason in the world than that she wanted her husband to make love to her, while his mind was filled with thoughts of another woman.

But it would be worse, far worse. She would go into his room at night, sit down on the edge of his bed. . . . I just thought I'd ask you, darling, hadn't I better order you some new shirts. . . . Or she would call him into her room when she was in bed. . . . Come in, dearest, I want to talk to you for a minute. I don't see enough of you these days, darling. . . .

She had the real things, the permanent things. They had made a success of their marriage, there could be no doubt of that. They were a very modern couple. She had men friends. Adrian was going to paint her portrait. She and Jay would live out their lives together. Every one would be able to see that they got on very well. They would have little jokes, amusing friends; courtesy, flattery, security. They would never quarrel, never nag or bicker. Lucia, my dear. Jay darling. My dear, you have never failed me. . . . She went to the window and leaned out into the silent night. Oh, my darling, she whispered, I never will.

xi

Again she pressed her fingers over her mouth. She was working herself up. She was tired, her self-control was shattered. She was deliberately making herself hysterical, just as Mamma used to do.

Stiffly she moved to her dressing case, and groped with crazily shaking hands for her bottles. It was late. She must go to bed. Some repetition of her familiar routine might calm her. She made a task of her preparations, sorting the things with elaborate care. She carried the bottles and jars to the bathroom, arranged them painstakingly on the glass shelf. Gradually, her breath came more evenly. She was insanely tired. In the morning she would be able to take a sensible view of things.

For to-night she was very unlike herself. She was behaving like a foolish, hysterical woman. People who looked for trouble always found it. Her imagination was over-active; she had always been nervous and apprehensive. Jay would be angry if he knew how she had distressed herself, how she had invented all sorts of tormenting ideas. Always she had felt that suspicion was vulgar. She had never allowed herself to indulge in jealous fancies.

But she had just been driving herself mad with suspicion. What else was it? She had built an elaborate structure, but it had no basis of proven fact. She was suspicious of Jay because his face was drawn and white, because she could see how he had suffered. But that was natural enough. Such a tragic accident to a friend would be a shock for any man. It need not mean that he had been deeply in love with the dead woman.

Suspicion, unsupported by proof, was the idlest self-indulgence. And what proof of Jay's infidelity had she, what proof that any one would value? Only a glimpse of a cigarette case caught in the swiftest oblique glance. Upon that instant of casual observation rested her entire accusation of Jay! She had been sure that it was her cigarette case. Yet, if she were called upon to swear in court that she *knew* she had seen it, would she be able to do so? Well, surely she would hesitate, if anything important hung on it.

But she had been willing enough to swear away her confidence in her husband, her life's happiness. She had undertaken to do that lightly enough. It grew more and more absurd, as she contemplated it.

And even if it had been the cigarette case, there might have been a simple enough explanation. Jay might have run across Mrs. Ennes quite accidentally on the street. Or he might have telephoned her to send it to him by a messenger, while he was downtown. There were all sorts of possible explanations. She had chosen to consider only the most unpleasant one. There was more of Mamma in her than she had realized.

xii

Lucia took a piece of cotton, and wet it in cold water, wringing it damp between clasped palms. She was almost calm now. Once more she was able to think clearly, rationally. She forced a wan smile at the reflection of her white, drooping face.

From the shelf she selected a silver-topped bottle and prepared to pour a fragrant liquid on the cotton pad. But the bottle slipped from her unsteady fingers, smashed with a tinkling impact on the tiled floor of the bathroom. Staring at the scattered fragments of the glass, the spreading liquid, she began silently to weep. The delicate perfume rose and vanished. Moments passed. But still Lucia stood painfully gazing at the bathroom floor. Still tears ran down her pale cheeks, as though hopelessly she grieved for the loss of some secret perfume which she had cherished.

The End